What Reviewers Are Saying

The Wedding Rescue:
Love in Little Tree, Book One
"a full-bodied romance filled
with a lot of emotional layers"
—Long and Short Reviews

Santa Dear
"an uplifting story"

Holly & Ivey
"Perfectly sweet Christmas romance!"

Stand-In Mom
"a charming romance"
—Romantic Times Book Reviews,
4 ½ Stars

"rich in emotional detail"
—Long and Short Reviews

Sign up for Megan's Readers' Group on her website,
MeganKellyBooks.com.

This one is for my kids.
Being your mom has been the joy of my life.

And as always, for my husband

Cover design by The Killion Group, Inc.

ISBN 978-0988601772

BABY MAKES THREE

Love in
LITTLE TREE

BOOK THREE

MEGAN KELLY

CHAPTER ONE

June

"'Bout time ya got here, boy."

Clint Walker eyed his uncle as he stepped into the church vestibule, admittedly running a little behind schedule. The drive from L.A. had been smooth, though it took longer than usual, since he'd planned out locations to stop and photograph landscapes. Some places he'd had to hike in to or wait for lighting, and a few times he'd discovered shots he hadn't planned, all of which took longer than anticipated.

And, as his luck ran, his crusty Uncle Crusty would be the first one to see him and badger him about his tardiness. He wore a white button-down shirt with suspenders to hold up his black pants, and a full white beard nearly hid his face, but no one would mistake him for kindly ol' Santa Claus.

"I'm not late," Clint told the crusty old man who had more than earned his nickname. "The rehearsal hasn't even started."

"Humph. Yore brother coulda used your help, had you been here."

Clint glanced into the church. The pastor stood talking to the father of the bride. No one else was in sight. Nothing seemed to be happening yet. "Help doing what?"

Crusty flung his hands out. "Wedding stuff. Don't try to put this on me that you wasn't here."

Making no sense, but obviously feeling justified, the old guy limped his uneven hitch-step up the aisle, grumbling. Clint's chest ached with love, and he nearly laughed with the joy of being home. Living in Los Angeles had its advantages career-wise, but more and more, he felt the pull to be back home in good ole Little Tree, Montana. "Nice to see you again, too," he called.

Doc Marshall and the pastor looked up. Both men raised a hand in greeting. "You're always welcome in God's house," the preacher said. "Be good to see you here more often."

"When I'm in town, pastor." Clint retreated down the hall, seeking out his brother, who had won the heart of one of the Marshall twins. Clint would have chosen the veterinarian twin for Jack, to help him out on the ranch. But Grace, Jack's choice of fiancée, must suit him in the "opposites attract" vein. As a newly-celebrated landscape painter, Grace would bring excitement and vibrancy to Jack's life—something starkly lacking in the past three years since his first wife passed away.

Hearing a conversation in one of the rooms, Clint tapped his knuckles against the door. When a male voice called to come in, he did just that.

Clint relaxed at the sight of his brother. Older by five years, Jack looked healthy and happy, which were the only things that mattered. Beside him stood his intended, a slim blonde in a cornflower blue dress that matched her eyes. Clint knew enough from his advertising work in L.A. to recognize designer fashion when he saw it. How would Grace take to ranch life? As a child, she'd been absorbed in her art, with a kind of not-really-present, dreamy demeanor.

Jack's face lit as he spotted him. "Clint. How was the drive?"

"Uncle Clint." The little girl's cry alerted him in time to plant his feet before Annabeth jumped into his arms, a blur of limbs and dark hair. At six, she could have knocked him backward without that last minute heads up.

He hugged her close, overcome with emotion. "You've grown, peanut."

She nodded, her black curls bouncing. "I'm six-and-three-fourths."

"Hardly seems possible." He'd missed so much of her life, only visiting briefly during the past two years. With a smooch, he set her to her feet and answered Jack.

"The drive went fine." They shook hands then hugged. Clint fought a wave of homesickness and covered it with an enthusiastic tone. "Am I late? A couple of the places I stopped to take pictures took longer than I intended. I got caught up in the light and scenery."

And perhaps his own sentiment for the land, but he didn't want to sound mushy.

"You're not late at all." Grace nodded at him. "I understand the delay if you were shooting."

"Thanks." Clint kissed her cheek. "You're looking lovely. Sure you want to take on this sourpuss?"

She shrugged. "Somebody has to."

"Well, then, I guess that's settled." He turned to Jack. "She's too pretty for you. You know that, right?"

"I do."

Grace arched her brows over teasing blue eyes. "You just be sure to say those words tomorrow."

"That's the plan."

"Good. I'm going to let you two talk. I need to check on Lexi. Make sure she got here from that calf she was—" Grace shuddered "—doing whatever to." She placed a hand on Clint's arm. "I'm coming out to the Rocking W for a while after the rehearsal dinner tonight. Are you still going to show me your portfolio?"

His stomach clenched. Believing in his talent was one thing; showing his photographs to a critical eye was wildly different. Her offer to look them over and give her honest opinion had meant a lot. Back in L.A. Now, as the moment for the big reveal rushed at him, he wanted to reconsider. But "nothing ventured" and all that. He swallowed his nerves. "Sure. I remembered."

"Good." She turned to Annabeth. "Come with me and see if your aunt-to-be has arrived."

Annabeth's grin showed all her teeth intact, which would look nice for the photos this weekend. "Aunt-to-be, aunt-to-be."

Grace gave Clint a quick hug. "Jack and I are both glad you're here. He may not admit it, but he's missed you."

Jack scowled at her back as she walked away with his daughter. "Don't go telling him stuff like that. He'll get a big head."

Clint grinned. "You've been hanging around Crusty too long."

"You're not wrong about that," Jack said. "That old cowboy is getting more cantankerous as the years pass."

"Hard to believe that's possible."

"It factored in to why I built us a separate house. It's a surprise wedding present for Grace."

Thrown like a greenhorn on his first bronc, Clint could only stare. "I understand why you'd want to get away from the old buzzard, but the family has always lived at the ranch house. As cramped as it's been, we've only had the one place for one hundred and fifty years."

"That's true, but he's the owner. Can you see him going easy on Grace, or see her putting up with him every day?"

Their mother had. Jack's first wife, Sarabeth, had. Could it be Crusty had become that much more argumentative, or did he just not get along with Grace? Or maybe Jack wanted to start this marriage in a place separate from memories of his first wife.

The news didn't sit right, but Clint would always support his brother. "I'm sure she'll be grateful. He's certainly not an easy guy to be around. But why hasn't she seen the new house?"

"Grace sticks to the ranch house when she comes. She's not one to wander."

"Don't you think she'll want input? She's a woman. And an artist."

"She can redecorate."

Clint shrugged. He'd meant placement of walls, design, number of rooms, not picture hangings. But Jack knew his fiancée better than Clint did. He only hoped Jack knew what he was doing.

Jack put a hand on Clint's shoulder for a second. "Thanks for being here."

"I'm your brother. Who else would be your best man? Crusty?"

Jack snorted.

"Exactly."

"I hope this isn't too hard on you. This is the first wedding you've been to since… Well, since."

Both men stood for a few moments, looking in opposite directions. An outsider might have thought they were comfortable with the silence. Bored even. Two tough, men-of-few-words types.

Instead, Clint's shirt chafed like new wool, and he had to fight not to fidget. He should have realized Jack would bring up Sheryl, Clint's ex-almost-fiancée, but until that moment, Clint hadn't associated his doomed relationship with a wedding. Their wedding never took place. For that matter, the proposal never took place.

But it was the first wedding he'd attended in the two years since Sheryl left him because he hadn't been ready to have a family…at twenty-three. After dating through college, they'd been on a predictable path toward marriage and family. Unfortunately, Sheryl had wanted to race toward the finish line while Clint took measured steps.

"Have you talked to her recently?" Jack shook his head. "Of course you have. I don't know why I even asked."

Clint didn't need to defend his actions, but he knew Jack worried about the situation, so he said quietly, "I'm still her friend."

"But not responsible for her problems."

Her ultimatum to start a family had worked against them. He'd stood firm, claiming they had plenty of time. They weren't even married yet, so what was the rush? She'd gotten mad, gotten pregnant by some jerk in a bar, and gotten in a car accident when Clint refused to marry her and raise the kid as his own.

"How is she?" The words seemed pulled out of Jack.

Clint hid a smile. Jack was so damn decent, concerned against his "better judgment" about the woman, because she'd once been the center of Clint's world.

"Back in rehab."

Jack nodded. "It's hard to kick pain meds. I'm watching Crusty. He isn't having any problems. But still…"

"Still."

Sheryl claimed she needed the pills, that they made things better, which Clint read as "zoned her out so she didn't have to deal with reality." She'd had her seatbelt on, but across her stomach rather than over her hipbones. The air bag explosion thrust the edge of the seatbelt into her abdomen, glass flew and sliced her skin, and metal from the door became embedded in her side. Sheryl's physical injuries had healed in the first year and she'd regained the ability to walk with a barely noticeable limp. But she lost the baby and her ability to become pregnant. And any reason to live, though she never said it aloud. The admission all but screamed out from her vacant eyes.

Doc Marshall stuck his head in the doorway. "Lexi's finally here, and the pastor's ready to start if you are."

Jack smiled, and no one would know they'd been having a serious conversation. "Very ready. I only wish the rehearsal was the actual ceremony and we could be done with this."

"Couldn't agree more," Doc said. "Can't wait to put all this festivity behind us and get back to normal life."

Clint shook his head at them. "I wouldn't tell Grace that."

Doc Marshall narrowed his eyes. "I'll deny every word."

The doc and Jack laughed and headed down the corridor. They were outdoor men, used to giving orders and leading others. Neither could be called a shrinking violet—unless the speaker ducked quickly afterward—but they didn't enjoy the spotlight. Working in advertising in L.A. had erased any trace of reserve Clint might have learned growing up on the ranch.

Lexi had indeed arrived, looking like her twin sister and very unlike her too in a simple flowered sundress. Grace resembled a porcelain sculpture with fine lines, while Lexi sparkled with the energy of a modern abstract. Everyone knew everyone else in Little Tree, so he wasn't surprised when she hugged him hello. "Hey, Clint. Looks like we're going to be brother and sister, sort of."

"That sounds right. Ready to get these two hitched?"

She shrugged. "It's hardly any work for me. Grace has every detail planned. All I have to do is show up."

"Me too."

"Don't keep Jack up all night partying."

Clint put a hand on his chest and widened his eyes. "Me? I have no control over that."

"Sure you do. You're the best man."

Clint leaned in. "Glad you noticed."

She chuckled.

"Clint." Jack's voice cracked like a gunshot in the echoing church. "Stop bothering Lexi and come stand where you're supposed to."

After a surprised glance at his brother, Clint turned to Lexi with a wink. "I'll see you after."

Perhaps nerves had grabbed hold of Jack. Clint stepped beside him. "I went to say hello. I didn't realize you needed me for anything."

"That looked more like flirting than just saying hi. Don't break her heart."

Clint smirked. "There's hello and then there's *hel-lo*. The little tomboy grew up to be stunning."

Jack shifted. "I'm aware."

Unable to keep from needling his older brother, Clint jabbed Jack's ribs with an elbow. "Does Grace know you're 'aware'?"

"They're identical twins." The exasperation in Jack's voice indicated Clint's teasing had hit its mark. "If one's beautiful, then the other is too."

"So we could each have a beauty on our arm, right?"

His brother sighed. "Look, Lexi's going to be my sister-in-law. It'll be awkward if you two have a fling and then have to face each other after you break it off. I don't want any tension in the family."

"Hey! What if she breaks my heart?"

Jack glared. "Don't take that chance." He walked over to Grace, clearly done being tormented by his younger brother.

Was it taking a risk on love again that had put a burr under Jack's skin? Because his brother was sure strung tight.

Clint had to grin. It felt good to be home.

He behaved throughout the wedding rehearsal, taking his instructions seriously. He'd served as Jack's best man the last time as well, but at seventeen, he'd been more nervous than the groom. This wedding eight years later found them standing at the altar as different men. Clint hoped he had more polish, while Jack had experienced a loss that would have broken him if he hadn't had a toddler to raise.

After the rehearsal, the small group gathered at Giovelli's Italian restaurant where they had a private room reserved. Despite Jack's earlier warning, Clint flirted with Lexi, who flirted right back. Jack's gaze burned down the table at him from time to time, but Clint simply smiled in return. Lexi regarded him as a friend, nothing more, and he admired her on the same level. Despite her breath-taking looks, he didn't feel a spark of desire. During the appetizer course, she entertained him with tales of ornery animals and equally-as-ornery ranchers, while he embellished his stories of life in the big city to entertain her.

They'd finished their salads when Lexi glanced over his shoulder and her face lit. "Rachel!"

Squeals erupted from the twins as they both jumped to their feet. Amused, Clint turned to see the newcomer.

And lost his breath.

"Who's that?" he managed after a few seconds.

But Lexi had already headed toward the woman. Perhaps she didn't hear his comment, as he hadn't had much air to voice it.

The two embraced, joined by Grace. While the blond twins lit the room, their companion sent a shock of awareness through his body. He sat unable to move, despite every cell yearning toward her. He'd never experienced a reaction this overwhelming. Golden highlights shot through her brown hair, adding to her natural glow. She laughed, and he wanted her by his side, sharing that sound with him. His world shifted like a funhouse floor at the state fair.

As Jack joined the women, Clint searched his memory for having ever met Rachel. There had been a relative who came to stay with the Marshalls during summers when they were kids, but he'd been too busy at the ranch helping Jack after their parents died to go into town much. He needed to correct his oversight now.

Glancing at the empty space beside him at the table, he pulled a chair up. Seated between Lexi and Rachel, he'd have a chance to get to know her through the women's conversation. Hopefully, he could guide her his way before someone showed her to the seat at the other end of the table—down by Doc Marshall, and worse, too far away from Clint—which had presumably been reserved for her.

Clint snagged a waiter to provide a place setting then walked over for an introduction. Up close, she could have been described as pleasant looking except for her stunning smile. Or her sparkling laugh. Her hair had been gathered into a neat bun at her nape, reminding him of a cinnamon roll. He could imagine eating her up. Clint would have scoffed if anyone mentioned love at first sight, but lust at first sight he totally believed in.

Grace turned to him as he approached. "And this is Jack's brother, Clint Walker. He's the best man."

Clint winked and extended his hand. "People keep saying that about me."

Jack snorted.

Rachel took his hand with hers. He wanted her soft, warm hand on his skin. Her confidence drew him closer, the way she looked him in the eye and gently laughed at his joke.

"I'm Rachel Marshall, just a cousin."

"Not just," Lexi objected. "Our only cousin." She pretend-glared at Clint. "That makes her like a sister to us, so you've been warned."

He gritted his teeth. Why did everyone talk to him as though he'd earned a reputation as a heart-breaker? Was the taint of L.A. so strong in their minds? "Then I'll pay her special attention." Turning back to Rachel, he crooked his arm. "I made a place for you at the table. May I escort you?"

She glanced down the table and spied the empty spot he'd provided. "Why, thank you, Clint."

His groin throbbed in response. He'd do more than this to please her if she'd let him. He set his mind to charming her, to influence the lady's mind away from his new and undeserved reputation as a player.

Fortunately, no one corrected him as to the seating arrangement before he rushed Rachel away. Lexi would sit one person from her—with him in the middle, and Grace had duties as the bride. His solution probably made things easier for the twins.

That was his story, anyway, if anyone asked.

"So, Lady Rachel, what do you do back in the kingdom from whence you came?"

She laughed as he pulled out her chair. "I'm a third grade

teacher."

"Oh, now, I doubt that." He held in a smile as her brows furrowed in confusion. "I'm sure you're a first-rate teacher."

Her laughter tinkled as though someone had rapped on a wine glass for a toast.

Tinkled? Oh, my God. He'd lost his mind. But gazing at her again, he decided he might not care. He was on vacation. A light flirtation would be a welcome counterpoint to Jack's serious mood.

"You're funny. I'm glad we're sitting together." She paused to smile up at the waiter as he brought her a salad. "I hope you aren't offended if I eat," she told Clint. "I spilled water on my snack in the car and I didn't want to stop to buy something else."

"Please. Go right ahead. Want me to—"

Feed you? he'd almost said. Good lord! He was in serious trouble with this one. "Get you a drink?" he finished instead.

She pulled the fork from her mouth and hastily chewed then swallowed. He'd asked at the exact wrong time, like an inconsiderate waiter. "Yes, please. I drank water all the way here. I'd appreciate some wine or tea or even lemonade. Something with a flavor to it."

"On it." He hated to leave her side, but he needed to find a real waiter. Wine, he decided.

Certainly not to get her inebriated, he assured his

conscience as he crossed the room. He'd never been that kind of guy, no matter how black the Marshall twins painted his reputation.

Returning with a bottle of wine, he filled their glasses.

Lexi shook her head when he offered. "I'm not officially on call, but then, Dad isn't either. If the phone rings, we're flipping a coin, so I better stay sober."

Clint frowned. "I can't imagine your clients would call. Everyone has always respected your dad. They could give him these two days, at least."

Lexi nodded. "They'll do their best, I'm sure, unless it's a real emergency they can't handle."

Rachel shook her head and sighed. "If only the animals could read the calendar. Then they'd know not to have babies or upset stomachs this weekend."

"It's a busy time of year," Lexi said. "How's Bella progressing? I'm hoping she holds off until Sunday, at the least."

"I haven't been out to the ranch yet." Clint turned to Rachel, glad of a legitimate reason to give her his attention. "Bella's foal was sired by a rascal named Marco, who had just enough . . . gumption after being gelded to do the job."

Rachel's eyes widened. "They can still get a mare pregnant?"

"Not usually," Lexi put in. "That's the whole point of

gelding. But it is possible, obviously."

"Marco's special," Clint added. "Jack's bursting with pride. Marco has been his favorite ride for a while, and he hated to geld him, but it didn't make sense to have a stallion working the cattle. The danged horse had too much fire for ranch work, or to be around the stable with Annabeth getting old enough to go out there alone."

Lexi continued the story about his niece's growing love for horses, and Clint gave up wooing Rachel. No man could flirt effectively while talking about castration.

Jack pushed back his chair, kissed Grace's forehead, and left the room with Doc Marshall. Had the talk about Bella jinxed their peaceful evening?

Lexi watched with a worried crease between her brows. "I hope it's nothing to keep him out late."

"Do you know who would call tonight?" Rachel asked.

Lexi shrugged. "Not anything major. We're on duty, though, and available. Tomorrow, we cross our fingers."

"Maybe your dad wants to have a fatherly chat with Jack," Clint suggested. "Threaten him a little."

Lexi chuckled. "That's probably it."

Waiters arrived with the main course, and Lexi turned to Annabeth on her far side to help her cut up her spaghetti.

Clint seized the opportunity to talk to Rachel and steer the conversation away from animal parts. "So, is there a Mr.

Rachel?"

He winced and she hid her laughter behind a napkin. *Real smooth.* This woman threw him off what little "game" he had.

"No, there's not." Her laughing blue eyes held his.

"Are the men in Colorado blind or just stupid?"

She sobered. "It's not them. I'm not in the market for a husband or boyfriend right now."

"Right now?" He took in her expression. "Recent breakup?"

"No. I'm way over the last guy, but he did make me realize it was time to take a break from dating. I have a bucket list, and dating is way down on…"

Clint tried to maintain an expression of polite interest and not laugh at her discomfort as she nearly bashed his entire gender.

Rachel blushed and ducked her head for a moment. "Sorry. That probably sounded rude. I just have something else, something important I want to accomplish in the next few months."

"Nothing wrong with that." Taking a chance, he traced one finger over the back of her wrist, watching as goose bumps formed on her arm. "Are you able to work on this 'something important' while on vacation? This weekend, I mean."

She grinned. "No. No, definitely not."

"Well, then, perhaps we could spend some time together?

I don't have a date for the wedding."

"What a coincidence. I don't have a date either."

Clint leaned toward her, a scant few inches separating his lips from hers. He lowered his voice. "Do you believe in coincidence?"

She shook her head. "Not usually, but I'm grateful for this one."

He held her gaze for a moment then leaned back in his chair. He could have sworn he heard her breath whoosh out, and he hid a pleased smile. Then he could have sworn in sheer frustration as his conscience poked him. He groaned. "I'm the best man."

She winked. "So I've heard."

Clint chuckled. "I have to take Jack out for his bachelor party later tonight."

"And I need to spend some time with my uncle and my cousins."

"Tomorrow?"

She bit back a smile. "Sorry, I have to go to a wedding."

"Right. I've heard there's a big shindig in town. So, come out to the ranch in the morning and we'll take a ride."

"I'd like that—if Grace doesn't need me."

He leaned toward her again, and this time she met him halfway. He could count every faint freckle, but this close, he only wanted to taste her lips. "There's always after the wedding."

"We can dance at the reception—when your duties allow, that is. I understand that you have a bridesmaid to attend to."

"It's just Lexi."

Rachel chuckled.

"I didn't mean it that way."

She touched his arm with her cool fingers. "I won't tell her."

His heart galloped at her touch. "Ah, a woman who can keep a secret. That's a good thing, right?"

Rachel just smiled.

The next afternoon, Clint glanced around the assembled wedding party in the church while he shot some candid pre-wedding photos. The personality-deficient photographer they'd hired insisted on taking the same stiff, static, lifeless shots every other couple had in their albums.

Clint hoped to see Grace's cousin. Rachel's dry humor had captivated him, and of course, she was sexy as hell. But he couldn't have a weekend fling with a woman from his sister-in-law's family, then head back to L.A. with fond memories. Too messy. However, he found he didn't want to stay away completely either. He'd limit their interaction to conversation and innocent flirtation due to the new family ties.

Once he found her.

He leaned over to whisper to Jack. The last thing he needed was anyone matchmaking. "Is their cousin coming?"

Jack slid him a glance. "Don't screw with her, little brother—in any sense."

"Just looking for someone to talk to." He aimed his camera lens at the bride's sister and snapped a shot of Lexi's laughing blue eyes. "I suppose I could chat up Lexi, but brothers interested in twins is a bit cliché."

Jack scowled. "Don't mess with Lexi, either."

The hard anger in his tone took Clint by surprise. "Hey, I wouldn't. I've always liked Lexi. Platonically," he tacked on when Jack turned to face him. "I would never hurt her or anyone in Grace's family."

Jack's shoulders fell into their usual non-aggressive lines. Hopefully the hair on the back of his neck relaxed as well. Sheesh. Jack should know him better than that. Clint wasn't a heart-breaker. He liked women, and, sure, he'd had quite a few dates after the end of his long-term relationship with Sheryl, but he never used anyone.

"So?" He couldn't stop himself from asking. "Is Rachel coming?"

Jack shrugged. "I don't think so. She's not in the wedding party. Just you and Lexi for witnesses."

Clint nodded, trying to appear uninterested, despite being *very* interested in the teacher from Colorado. Besides him and

Lexi, only Grace's father and Jack's daughter accompanied the bridal couple and the pastor. "I'll catch up with Rachel later then."

"Or not."

"Or not." Clint nodded his agreement then grinned, unable to stop himself from bedeviling his brother. Another drawback to living so far away. "Or a lot."

Jack growled and walked over at the photographer's beckoning.

And what a piece of work the photographer was. He'd better produce exceptional prints because his disdainful exchanges with the bridal party indicated he'd rather be elsewhere—like ordering around his Minions.

Clint took another few shots of the church architecture and glass windows, and more candids of his family, which would expand in a few hours, after the wedding. He couldn't have been more thrilled that his brother had found someone to fill his heart and to mother his child. Jack had lost the love of his life and hadn't looked for a replacement. Clint had been in L.A. when Grace returned from her tour of the world, where she spent several years improving her art. He'd missed watching his brother fall in love, and could only send up a prayer of thankfulness. His brother would marry, have more children, and eventually inherit the ranch.

In a rare phone call, Crusty had told Clint about his

surprise for Jack. Following tradition, the plan had been for Crusty to name Jack as heir once Crusty went toes up. But the old man had made a different arrangement, which he would present to the wedding couple tonight at the reception. Jack's life would finally develop into a happy family portrait, complete with ranch and homestead. Maybe Crusty could move into the new house.

Clint's shoulders tightened and he shook off his dissatisfaction. Jack getting married only underscored Clint's isolation in southern California. While his bosses valued his work, advertising no longer presented a challenge for him, or at least, not the challenge he yearned for. Great photos waited around every corner, but he couldn't support himself by taking pictures. Just by chance, he'd sold one of his photos to his boss to use in a campaign. But right now, working in advertising meant staying in L.A. where his connections were.

He was alone. His own fault, since on his last date, he'd spent more time photographing the scenery than talking to the very patient and kind woman he'd dragged along on a hike.

The time had come for a change. At twenty-five, he could still take chances in his career. He just had to shake off his ranch-learned conservatism and branch out into photography full-time.

He swallowed. The risk both scared and excited him.

CHAPTER TWO

After the pastor introduced Mister and Missus Walker to the congregation, Clint took Annabeth's hand and followed Jack and Grace down the aisle. He guided her to the bride's dressing room where he needed to sign the license. Lexi had gotten so sick sometime that afternoon, she couldn't attend her twin's wedding. Kevin had gone to recruit Rachel as the other witness.

His body recognized Rachel's voice before his brain did, sending prickles of awareness over his skin. He had a scant moment to gather himself to see her, as her voice came from the corridor directly outside the room. He hadn't been able to take her riding that morning since Bella chose to deliver her foal. He and Jack had been at her side for most of the night, in the strangest of bachelor parties. Today he'd been occupied, first with the foal, then the pre-wedding photos, and Rachel seemed to be more reserved than when they'd parted at the restaurant the evening before.

"Of course I'll sign as a witness, Uncle Kevin. I'd be

happy to. But then shouldn't one of us go check on Lexi?"

Clint's breath shallowed out as Rachel stepped into the room. She shimmered in an ultramarine dress that both hid and revealed her body in shadows and glimmers of deep blue. The satiny texture drew his gaze to her bare shoulders, which he wanted to caress. He took a visual trip down her modestly covered cleavage, his imagination tracing a path between her breasts. She had an attractive body, not skinny like the starving starlets in L.A. His journey continued to her exposed calves, sidetracked by the idea of sliding the uneven hem on that silky material upward. She was a vision. He sent a mental apology to Lexi for being glad Rachel had to step in as witness.

The photographer snapped a picture, nearly blinding the room as the groom signed the license. Jack blinked and held the pen in Grace's general direction. The pastor indicated the correct place and she signed.

"Yay!" Annabeth clapped, making everyone laugh. The camera flashed again, then twice more as Clint and Rachel signed as witnesses. Clint thought he'd hang himself if he had to resort to taking clichéd photographs for a living.

Rachel hugged Grace. "Congratulations, honey."

Clint slapped Jack on the back. "Good job. Now, I'm taking advantage of tradition by kissing the bride. I figure it's unlikely you're going to let me do it later."

"You figure right."

Clint dipped Grace backward. Her gasp made everyone laugh, followed by Jack's growl when Clint kissed her. Clint swung her upright and clapped a hand to his heart. "Damn, you're one lucky man, Jackson Walker."

Jack slid a proprietary arm around his bride's waist. "I know it."

She ducked her head, ill at ease in a way Clint never would have associated with Grace. He thought she'd play along when he dipped her for that kiss, but she'd been stiff and too serious.

He turned to Rachel, hiding his hope behind a joke. "Your turn?"

Rachel's eyebrows rose. "I've never heard of any custom where the witnesses kiss."

He smiled with wicked humor. "Every custom starts somewhere."

"Tempting, but no."

"I'll kiss you, Uncle Clint," Annabeth said.

They laughed. It seemed to him Grace's laughter was forced, but he shook off his worry. No one else noticed anything wrong.

"Best offer I've had all day." Best one he was likely to get too, he feared. He swung the girl up into his arms, and she kissed his cheek with a loud smack. He slid Annabeth back to her feet and shook his head at Rachel. "You had your chance."

Grace gave a tight smile. "We should go."

"Right," Jack said.

"Daddy, can I ride in the limo with you and Mommy?"

Clint choked back the lump in his throat, caught by surprise. Of course Grace would be Annabeth's stepmother now. He just hadn't expected the blow when he heard Jack's first wife being replaced as "Mommy." Though sweet Sarabeth would have wanted Jack and their daughter to find happiness again.

As moments ticked by, he realized the others hadn't moved either. Had Annabeth bestowing this title blindsided everyone?

Rachel shifted her weight, the first to recover. Perhaps since she hadn't known Sarabeth personally, she wasn't as affected. "Not this time, Annabeth. We'll get to the party faster than they will if we ride in my car."

"But I want to ride in the limo."

Jack stroked Annabeth's hair with a hand that trembled a little. "Not tonight, sugar cube. Tonight is for the bride and groom."

As the happy couple left the church, Clint sought to distract his niece. "I'll take you to the reception, Annabeth. We'll put the roof down on my car so you can feel the air rush through your hair."

"Can we go real fast?"

He laughed at his precocious niece and her rapid mood change. "You bet."

But he'd take his time with Rachel, given the chance. He turned to her. "Want to ride with us?"

"I have my own car. And you, sir, already have your hands full with this young lady." She smiled down at Annabeth.

Which kept her from seeing his reaction as his brain flooded with images of his hands being full of Rachel. He cleared his throat. "Maybe later."

She glanced at him and he realized he'd spoken aloud.

"Sounds good. I'd love to go for a ride in the moonlight." She paused and held his gaze. "With the top down."

He gulped and watched as Rachel left the room ahead of him.

Hot damn.

Clint spotted Rachel by the side door to the ballroom where the wedding reception should be starting any minute. People enjoyed the wine and hors d' oeuvres—but the bridal couple had yet to arrive. Annabeth spun in circles with a friend on the dance floor while the crowd milled around, restless. Pictures after the ceremony shouldn't take this long, especially since they'd shot the majority of them that afternoon before the wedding.

Except for the frown between her brows, Rachel looked as radiant as a bride herself. Clint scowled. That frown had been caused by his brother and Grace, the ingrates.

"Have you heard anything?" he asked as he approached her in the doorway.

"No."

"Damn it. Where are they? This isn't like Jack. He's usually dependable. Boring, actually."

Rachel's expression lightened. "I'm afraid Grace has been a bad influence then. She's anything but dependable. Or boring. When I offered to check on Lexi, Uncle Kevin said he had already, so I don't think they'd have gone to see her. The twins are close, but this is Grace's wedding day."

"Right. It seems unlikely."

"Excuse me." A waiter appeared from the kitchen area. They stepped out into the hallway with him.

"What can we do for you?" Clint asked.

Surprise flared on Rachel's face. Maybe he should have let her address the caterer, but he hadn't pegged her as one who separated duties by gender. Though, as cousin to the bride, maybe she had more territorial rights regarding the reception than a member of the groom's family.

The waiter cleared his throat and prattled on about serving dinner.

Clint glanced at Rachel, indicating he would let her handle

it. He tuned out the conversation, less concerned with feeding the guests than with Jack's whereabouts. In another few minutes, Clint would try Jack's cell phone again. He didn't want to interrupt the newlyweds presumably consummating their marriage, but almost the entire town waited to congratulate them. Jack knew as well as anyone that ranchers had little patience and less time to waste. And when it was time to party, they liked to cut loose.

"Thanks," Clint echoed as the waiter left. "It doesn't seem right to serve the wedding dinner without Jack and Grace."

Rachel shrugged. "The guests are here and the food is ready. The badly-behaving couple can eat when they get here. After they've apologized and explained where they've been."

"Maybe they're celebrating their marriage," he teased, pretty darn sure that was the case.

"They could have waited."

"Oh, sweetheart." Clint shook his head with a sad smile. "If that's what you think, you haven't been made love to properly."

She arched an eyebrow, but the shiver across her skin canceled out her imperious expression. "Is that right?"

"That's so right." He traced a finger across her shoulder, pleased to see a trail of goose bumps in the wake of the path. He lowered his voice and leaned closer, making the conversation more private. More direct. Speaking from his need to hers. "A Walker man knows how to please a woman."

Rachel gulped audibly. She tilted her head and dropped her gaze to his mouth before looking into his eyes again.

His breathing raced as his blood rushed south.

She put a hand on his chest and lowered her voice. "That sounds promising."

"I can promise you an unforgettable night." His mouth closed on hers, her lips soft and yielding. Dark and mysterious, smooth but with an undertone, he enticed her to discover more facets of need. When he lifted her against him, her arms circled his neck. His tongue teased her, stroked, retreated. He didn't want to crush her but—

Oh, hell yes, he did. He needed her closer. Even the thin layers of clothes between them were an irritation.

Rachel broke back, panting. He kept his body pressed to hers, not ready to lose their connection.

She glanced around the doorway into the room then back to survey him with a critical eye. "How old are you?"

He blinked in surprise. He hadn't been carded at a bar for years, and he'd judged her to be about the same age. "I'm twenty-five. Why?"

She loosened her embrace. "Shouldn't we be taking care of the guests?"

Had she not felt the same yearning? One glance at her flushed cheeks reassured him. Rachel had lapsed back into "family helper" mode for some reason, but desire hovered near the surface. He'd just have to draw it out again.

"They all have drinks." He kissed the corner of her mouth. "They're about to have dinner." He feathered his lips across her cheek. "There's nothing we can do for them."

"We should search for Grace and Jack."

Did her objection sound half-hearted or was that just hopeful hearing?

"We've all called." He traced a finger along her bottom lip, anticipating nibbling on it. "They don't want to be bothered."

"We should be doing something helpful."

"Short of knocking on the door to the honeymoon suite and dragging them out of bed like Victorian prigs, I don't see what more we can do."

"They're being irresponsible."

Clint brought his lips against hers again. "Let's be irresponsible too." He whispered the suggestion across her smooth hot cheek, breathing in the scent of heady flowers. Jasmine? Gardenia? Something intoxicating.

The sharp ping of someone tapping a glass broke the spell. Rachel turned and stiffened. They stepped into the ballroom to see the guests had gathered around Doc Kevin.

"He must have news." Clint cupped her shoulders as he stood behind her and leaned down to whisper reassurance in her ear. "It must be good news, though. He wouldn't announce it like this otherwise."

She relaxed and Clint pulled her against him for support. *Don't let it be bad news*. His muscles tightened as he waited for the murmurs to die down.

"Thank you all for coming," Doc Kevin said. "And thank you for your patience. I've just heard from…that naughty girl of mine."

The guests laughed. The vet's light delivery eased the tension from Clint's muscles. As soon as he made sure his brother and Grace were safe, he planned to kill Jack for worrying everyone.

Doc gave the reassurance Clint needed, encouraging everyone to stay and enjoy the evening. The guests cheered and Doc raised his glass. "To our hosts."

Glasses clinked, and everyone began talking—probably about Jack, which he would hate. Served him right. "At least they're okay."

Rachel blew out a breath. "Yes, thank goodness."

Waiters trooped past them with plates of steaming beef tenderloins, mashed potatoes drowning in butter, and asparagus spears gleaming beside glazed carrots.

"Jack triumphed in the food war," Rachel said, probably as off-balance as Clint felt. The good news had come with lousy timing, severing their connection. "I know Grace wanted something more exotic. She ran ideas past me and Lexi for weeks."

"There's asparagus, though. Jack can't stand the stuff."

She leaned back against him. "He's never had it prepared by a master."

Did she emphasize that last word or had desire messed with his hearing?

"An experienced chef could have made his knees weak."

Clint's mouth fell open, sure now that she was flirting. Leading him on, but he was a willing follower. Her words seemed ordinary, but her tone carried all the meaning he required.

She turned to him and ran a hand down his tie, stopping where his lapels met at his sternum. His heart thundered under her palm. "It should be tender."

He gulped. Behind her, no one paid them any attention.

Rachel traced a finger across his mouth. "Warm."

He licked his lip, tasting the slight salt of her touch, just missing nabbing her finger as she drifted it across to his cheek.

"And buttered," she added.

"You don't say?" He cleared the rasp of desire from his voice—and improper images from his mind. He needed a clear head. "Why don't you check with your uncle? See if he needs you. I'll go get my car."

"Are you going someplace?" She damn near batted her

lashes at him.

Her flirting gave him a solid green light. He held her upper arms, and she balanced against him with her hands on his chest. He hoped the gleam in her eyes indicated desire. Hadn't he decided he needed to take more chances in his life? Well, she was a risk, all right. One he would eagerly accept.

"Come with me, Rachel."

"To bed?"

"Yep."

"Right now?"

"Yep."

She swallowed. "I feel bad about leaving Uncle Kevin to handle all this alone."

"He's not alone. Mrs. Browning is supporting him. And who's wiser than a librarian? He'll be fine. What do you say?" Clint held his breath as excitement battled with impatience. "Want to come to bed with me?"

Rachel's smile grew saucy and she uttered the only word he needed to hear.

"Yep."

One last time, she would have sex without a reason. For the sheer fun of it. A fling. A taste of being young—she was still in her twenties, after all, at least for a few more days—and free.

Rachel eyed Clint at the wheel of his car. The convertible

had probably played havoc with her wedding hairdo, but the vehicle matched the carefree joy she felt tonight.

What happens in Little Tree stays in Little Tree.

She smirked. While no one would compare the small Montana town to the bright lights of Sin City, the motto fit her mood. She would take this one night off from worries, take a break from planning every second and every emotion of her life, and just enjoy this outrageously handsome man. He wanted her, she wanted him, and for tonight, that was all she would let matter.

Thank goodness he knew the way to Uncle Kevin's house because she'd been staring more at him than paying attention to streets. How could she give directions with this cowboy Adonis distracting her? Wheat-blond hair she wanted to run her fingers through. A tanned, square jaw she wanted to lick. Green eyes she wanted to watch turn black with desire. Big hands she wanted to feel caressing her body. She just *wanted* him. She never let her emotions decide her actions . . . Until tonight. Until Clint.

Too soon, and not nearly soon enough, the car stopped in front of her uncle's house. She opened the car door right before he reached it, and when she climbed out, mere inches separated them. She stood in his arms, where she wanted to be. She ducked her head, preferring not to kiss him here on the street, deserted though it seemed. This was her last crazy act, a private memory to be cherished in the years to come.

She retrieved the spare key from the mailbox.

"That's the first place I'd have looked," Clint said, "if I was trying to break in."

"Really?" Rachel gave the door a shove with her shoulder, loosening the seal on the jamb, slightly aslant in its old age. "I'd have looked under the doormat."

Clint followed her in. Moonlight and memory guided her to a table lamp. The dim light suspended them in a universe without time. Nothing mattered. No outside world existed. Just this man and this encounter.

"Is Lexi here?" he whispered.

"She and Grace have their own house. We're all alone." She walked back to him and slid her fingers up his chest. He caught her hands against him and held her captive. Captivated.

"I want to make love to you," he said.

Throat thick with emotion, she could only nod. Pulling her tight against him, he kissed all breath from her body and all thought from her mind. She nearly lost her balance—his kisses actually made her dizzy—and tried to save face by turning her fumble into the first step toward the stairs. She took his hand, its hard warmth both thrilling and settling her, and led him up to the guest bedroom.

She turned to him, the light from the hallway her only guide. That, and her overwhelming need to be near him, a need that drew her as though she were shards of iron and he was polar north. Stilling his hand on his top button, she shook her head. "Let me."

The burn in Clint's eyes as he surrendered to her touch sent spikes of feminine power to her core. Gaze locked on his, she popped one button, then another, then another, slowly, and even slower. A wicked playfulness built inside her as his sexual frustration stretched.

"Woman," he said in warning, "you better hurry this along."

"No."

He growled at her simple refusal, captured her hands, and brought her fists to his mouth. His top teeth settled onto her knuckle, and a frisson of lust swept over her. Despite not hurting her, he soothed her hand with a wet kiss anyway, his tongue swirling over the abused area. "Think what I could do with my tongue if you move a little faster."

Her privates clenched and went wet. "Trying to tempt me?"

"God, I hope so."

"No, it's a good idea." She rushed through the last button and spread his shirt. Before he could move, she opened her mouth over his pec, flicking his nipple with her tongue. His sharp inhale rewarded her efforts. She had only a moment to devour his chest with her gaze before she grazed his skin with her teeth. Her hands grasped his ribs, fingers digging in to hold him still, to keep him close. As she moved to the other side of his hard muscled chest, he eased her back. "My turn."

She anticipated watching his expression as he unzipped her, but he turned her around. Frustrated, she couldn't see as his fingers located the zipper tab. Disappointment jolted through her. She'd expected more of him than fast and obligatory foreplay. *Just get it over with then.* His fingertips brushed her shoulders and goose flesh burst across her skin. The zipper descended and he trailed a finger along the opening, a faint touch that tightened her nipples.

She'd been wrong. Not being able to see him only heightened her senses, made the feeling more intense.

When the zipper reached her waist—*just about there, another inch, hurry*—his tongue touched the nape of her neck and sizzled coolly down her spine, lapping into the valley between each vertebrae. The zipper stopped at her tail bone; Clint did not. He peeled the dress down her torso while licking her skin. When she sucked in air, the dress pooled at her feet.

Her strapless bra fell off before she realized he had unhooked the clasp. His hands came around and cupped her breasts as he kissed the bend at the side of her waist—a surprisingly erotic spot, she learned, as a shudder of need overtook her. He turned her slowly toward him, kissing, kissing his way up to her breasts, dragging his tongue in a path so deliberate her nipples ached before his mouth even touched them. Her skin quivered in anticipation. After teasing him, she could only imagine the delicious torture he'd inflict.

She could hardly wait.

Maddeningly, he did make her wait. His hands skimmed over her, igniting need but not satisfying it. He would caress and tease, then move on. All the while, he sucked at her breasts until her desire built to a point she could barely stand. When he knelt before her, she had to hold on to his shoulders. When he nudged her legs open, when his tongue touched her intimately, her vision went white. She cried out as tremors shook her.

He laid her gently back on the bed and settled beside her, propped up on one arm to glance into her face. His hand made free with her body, trailing fire and ice along her nerve endings. "I'm going to apologize now. This first time might be hasty."

This first time? He hadn't been paying attention, but she liked the promise of more. She felt greedy—they hadn't even finished round one yet and she was anticipating the next. Grabbing his hand, she brought his fingers to her lips and playfully sunk in her teeth. "I can't wait either. Enough with the foreplay."

He laughed. "You might be the perfect woman."

After suiting up for protection, he entered her, slowly, watching her face as she spread herself and guided him in.

She wanted to close her eyes, to concentrate on the sensations, on the moment. But at the same time and equally or even more important, she wanted to watch Clint, to be with *this man* by touch, taste, sight, scent—

And *oh!* To hear him groan her name. Whether she wanted to watch him or not didn't matter, for she only saw stars exploding in the darkness as she climaxed.

Rachel nestled into Clint, feeling languid and sated. She luxuriated in the feel of him spooned behind her, his strong hard muscles a convenient support as she lay boneless against him. Warm and content, she pressed the arm encircling her closer into her ribs.

"I don't have one-night stands." The words burst from her. She didn't want Clint to regard this as a habit of hers. She liked him and cared about his good opinion.

"Me neither."

"No, seriously. Longmont isn't that small of a town, but our current school board is ultra conservative. At the beginning of the year, the teachers received a memo suggesting we not buy our liquor in a grocery store where students or parents could see the bottles in our baskets. We're to be role models, of course, but the school board expects us to be almost inhumanly perfect."

"Where do they suggest you buy your pot?"

Giggling, she smacked his arm. "They don't, despite it being legal. I'm sure they'd suggest we sneak into Denver wearing disguises."

He rose and tilted her shoulders onto the pillows to see her face. "Their attitude is a bit rigid, but it shouldn't be a problem for you." He nuzzled her neck, making her breasts go heavy. His mouth burned a path to her nipples, which stood out in invitation. She'd have thought it too soon to be roused again. Her body proved her wrong.

Her breath caught and her head fell back as he flicked her nipple with his tongue. Sucked it into his mouth. Tugged with his teeth.

She grasped his head, holding him to her as she slid down on the bed. All thoughts of the stodgy school board flew away. A problem for another day.

Waking from a slight doze, Rachel glanced at movement in the bedroom doorway, surprise turning to pleasure at the sight. Was there anything sexier than a man bearing a tray of food?

"You shouldn't have, but I'm glad you did." She scooted over on the bed, dragging the sheet up over her breasts. Eating naked made her self-conscious. He quirked a brow at her. "I know," she said. "It's silly, considering what we've been doing. Just…oh, shut up."

He grinned and slid in beside her. "I've seen your breasts."

"You're one to talk. You put on your boxers."

"Hey, I was in the kitchen. I might have run into the doc."

Her eyes went wide with panic. "Is he home?" she whispered.

"Hey, Doc!" Clint shouted, then after a moment said, "I guess not."

She narrowed her eyes. "Not. Funny."

"Ooh, Miss Schoolteacher." He clasped his hands to his chest. "Are you going to punish me? Keep me after class—just you and me in a dark room?" He waggled his eyebrows. "Please?"

Rachel laughed. "No."

He dropped his act. "You *are* mean. Can I ply you with cheap wine?"

"Sure. But knowing Uncle Kevin, it'll be good."

"The doc knows his wine?" Clint unwrapped foil from the bottle. "Huh. A cork."

"Uncle Kevin started buying wine to support a friend who dabbled in grapes and wildflower wines. You'd have to ask him who. Anyway, that got him interested in the process, and by the time his friend became bored with wine making, Uncle Kevin was hooked. Not in a bad way. Not an alcoholic."

Not like his brother, dear old Dad. She grimaced. Dad

didn't stick around to raise her and he definitely didn't belong in her happy moment.

"I know what you meant. The doc is solid." Clint poured white zinfandel into the glasses he'd brought upstairs. He tapped his to hers. "To the doc, and his hopefully excellent taste in vino."

After they sipped the bold freshness, he said, "This is good. I'll have to remember it. You and Doc Kevin seem close. You used to visit for summer vacations, right?"

"Yeah. Things at home...weren't great. Uncle Kevin always felt responsible or guilty or something because my dad was his brother and Dad wasn't...well, a stellar guy. Uncle Kevin's probably the only man I can say I truly admire. Raising Grace and Lexi after his wife died wasn't easy. Being an involved citizen. Taking care of his business. Staying true to his values."

Clint raised his glass again with a nod of respect. "To the doc."

"So," she continued after a sip, "I came here and gained two sisters every summer. As an only child, that made leaving my friends in Longmont bearable. By the time my visit ended, I didn't want to go back home."

"Isn't that always the way?"

She assembled a cheese and cracker sandwich and held it out to Clint. He swooped in and engulfed it, including her fingers. She pulled them back with a laugh and wiped them on a napkin.

"The best part is tasting you." He held her gaze.

Heat rushed over her cheeks and downward as a tingle of arousal tickled her belly. "You've had enough of me, as I recall."

"Oh, I recall too, vividly, but I wouldn't say enough. Not yet."

"No?"

"This is sustenance. Strength for Round Two. Or" —he grinned— "would it be Three?"

Ignoring the fire in her cheeks, she locked her gaze on his. "It would."

His expression intensified at her honesty.

"It will be." She watched his green eyes darken. "As soon as we regain some strength and get to it."

"Yes, ma'am." He shoved a cracker in her mouth then two in his own.

God, he was cute. Sexy. Fun.

He moved the tray to the floor. She trailed her gaze over his muscled back, tingling in anticipation as she drank in the sight of so much male beauty.

The perfect guy to be her last fling.

CHAPTER THREE

The next day, Clint woke invigorated, despite having snuck out of the doc's house around midnight. Rachel hadn't wanted her uncle to find him there, and Clint hadn't been too keen on facing the doc either. Being consenting adults didn't mean squat when faced with the woman's family.

He saddled up and took a ride as the sun rose and then spoke with the men about the day's work. They didn't need his input, of course, but it felt good to talk ranching, to take responsibility, and to help out Jack.

When his brother stepped over the threshold with his bride, Clint felt the first niggle of unease. Jack set her down and kissed her cheek. Her cheek. *I kissed more than Rachel's cheek last night, and I'm not even in love with her.*

"If that's the best he can do," Clint said, walking down the hall toward them, "you might as well run away with me right now."

Jack shot upright like a hot poker had been inserted in his backside. Crusty hobbled out to greet them. "You gonna stand in the doorway for the rest of yore married lives?"

"Hello, Chris," Grace said.

Clint's jaw dropped along with Jack's and Crusty's. No one had called their uncle anything but Crusty in so long, Clint almost forgot he had another name. Crusty scolded her in his gruff way, ensuring that no one would make that mistake again.

Jack didn't stand up for Grace, didn't tell Crusty to back down, didn't laugh off her mistake to defuse the tension. Clint tried to shrug it off. Maybe Jack had picked up on the emotion in Crusty's voice. Their dad had called their uncle a few names during one of their arguments, most of them unrepeatable, and fortunately, "Crusty" was the one that stuck. The nickname tied Chris back to his brother, and the old buzzard wouldn't appreciate losing that link.

Or maybe Jack didn't want to argue with Crusty on the first day of his new life with Grace. Clint didn't envy his brother juggling all the compromises they'd have to make to manage the place with a woman in the mix. Their housekeeper had been the only feminine influence around here since Jack had been widowed. Clint didn't envy Grace either, trying to find her way in this maze of men. He hoped Jack realized she'd need his help.

They trailed into the kitchen after Crusty, no one commenting on how hard it was for hi to walk without the cane he was too stubborn to use. Seeing him struggle made Clint's heart pang. The feisty geezer was the bedrock of the Rocking W.

Clint decided to move things along. Crusty had a surprise up his sleeve, and the sooner he presented it, the sooner Crusty could grab a nap or at least get off his feet. "Hey, I should get on the road."

Jack hugged him, giving him a hard thump on his back to hide his emotion. Or to disable Clint from being able to drive off—one of the two. "Thanks for coming, little bro."

Clint chuckled at being called "little," since he stood as tall as Jack, but the comment had more to do with affection than age or height. "Wouldn't have missed it. I didn't have to do much as your best man as it turned out, but it was an honor."

"I'll return the favor someday."

"I'm in no hurry to give up my freedom." Realizing that sounded rude, Clint inclined his head toward the bride. "No offense, Grace."

"Have a safe trip." She kissed his cheek.

She'd complimented his portfolio the other night and recommended galleries on his route home, suggesting he mention her name to open doors. Helping him make connections in the art world was an unexpected bonus—after all, she'd already brought Rachel into his life. To show appreciation for his new sister-in-law, he said, "I plan to stop at those galleries you mentioned."

Grace blinked then smiled. "Oh. Good. I wish you luck."

Clint glanced at Crusty, anticipation of their reaction to the surprise welling in him. "Well, now, I'm not leaving quite yet. I didn't stay around only to make sure you left the hotel, you know."

Crusty retrieved the manila envelope he'd tucked behind the coffeemaker earlier that morning after showing the contents to Clint. "I been waiting to give you this. Woulda done it last night in front of ever'body, but you couldn't bother to come to yore own damned party." He ignored the warning glance from Jack. A smile split his white mustache apart from his close-shaved beard. "Happy wedding day, boy. And you too, Grace."

Jack stared at the document.

"What is it?" Grace asked at his side.

Clint whooped, unable to contain his excitement. "It's the deed to the ranch."

Their father had run the ranch as Crusty's foreman, expecting his sons to inherit one day since Crusty had never married and no woman claimed her children were his. Jack stood next in line to run the ranch when Crusty passed, though they weren't in a hurry to see that happen. But Crusty had decided to give them the ranch now. Jack held the fulfillment of their father's dreams in his hands. The continuation of the family legacy was now Jack's responsibility, one he'd earned through dedication and sheer hard work.

And the happy couple looked like they might be having seizures.

Taken aback by their graying color, Clint glanced over at Crusty to see if the old man had noticed Jack and Grace's strange reactions.

If a man could swagger while standing still, Crusty had the motion down pat. "It's a done deal, all legal-like. I signed it over to the both of you together in honor of the occasion. So don't go getting divorced."

Leave it to Crusty to invite the specter of doom to their party.

"To both of us?" Grace squeaked. "Wow. Thank you, Crusty."

Squeaked? What the hell? Everyone in Little Tree acknowledged Grace as the person with the most poise and sophistication to ever come from their small town. She had gained the respect of the art world, painting landscapes that brought critical acclaim and lucrative financial benefits. Why would this bit of good news unsettle her?

Why did Jack look like someone had handed him a dead rattler rather than the realization of his fondest dream? Actually, Clint *had* handed him a dead rattler back when they were kids, and Jack hadn't looked this unnerved. What was going on with the newlyweds?

Clint watched his brother and new sister-in-law, standing side by side but somehow not together. The gift should have had them hugging each other, with Jack dancing her around the kitchen. Clint started to feel less convinced of their love match. But why would Jack have married Grace otherwise?

After Jack and Grace expressed their thanks—rather stiffly, in Clint's opinion, Crusty said to Jack, "I waited till you were settled again. Now you need to start having some boys to run the place after yore gone. So hang on to this filly, boy, and get her to breeding."

Clint winced and shook his head. One day a wife and Grace was already being pressured to get pregnant. He jumped in, trying to sidetrack the conversation. "Only a dumb-ass would let loose of this pretty lady. And Jack may have been thrown on his head a time too often, but even he isn't that dim-witted."

His brother glared at him by way of appreciation while Grace went on about girls being as capable as boys to run a ranch. "My sister could run this ranch if she wanted to."

Jack smiled. "I have no doubt about that."

"Where is Lexi, anyway?" Clint asked. She must be recovered by now or one of them would have mentioned her illness.

Grace froze, eyes so wide he could almost peer into her brain. She stared up at her husband, who looked dazed, as if a steer had kicked him in the head.

Clint's Spidey senses tingled. Something was going on here, and it wasn't honeymoon hangover. He listened to them mumble excuses and wonder aloud where Lexi might be. Clint wanted to suggest he call Rachel and ask over at the doc's house. He hesitated though, not wanting to use Lexi's illness for his own benefit. He'd think of another reason to call Rachel before he left town. Maybe a quick bite at the diner before they each hit the road?

Grace made mimosas and they all toasted the wedding couple and Crusty's gift. Clint studied Jack and Grace while they clinked glasses. They acted stiff and awkward, like even drinking to a toast took a concentrated effort. Something smelled fishy. Could they have had a fight already?

"One other thing. I'm moving out," Crusty said, mentioning the cottage Jack had intended to move his small family into.

Grace protested Crusty's decision. The old man's news even overshadowed Jack's surprise of building them a house.

"As the owners of the ranch now," Crusty said with a stubborn set to his jaw, "you should live in the main house."

Jack shrugged, looking uncomfortable to have the new house mentioned again. "I didn't know the old coot planned to leave us the land."

"But even so," Clint said, eyeing Grace's white fingers gripping the chair back, "it would be nice to have that extra privacy. I've heard newlyweds like to run around naked."

He continued to watch the "happy" couple, doubt and anxiety churning in his gut. Familiar with all Jack's mannerisms, Clint noted his brother's discomfort, his scowling at nothing, his edginess. The man was hiding something, and not very well. Clint just had to figure out what. He reviewed every interaction between Jack and Grace since the wedding, which seemed the pivotal point when things changed.

When the answer came to him, Clint thought he'd lost his own mind. He had to know if he'd guessed right—and hoped he hadn't. He started the goodbyes again, a pang of longing hitting him as he hugged his brother and uncle. Up close, he took in Grace's sweet open nature and felt a rock settle in his gut. He was sure now.

He manipulated Jack out to the barn on the pretext of checking on the condition of one of the horses. Once out of earshot of the house and the ranch hands, he turned to Jack. "What the hell is going on?"

Clint pulled onto Rachel's street in Longmont, Colorado, convinced he was on a fool's errand. Well, it fit, since he'd become a fool the night he'd met her. He never had a one-night stand. Making love was a way to connect, and he had to know a woman before he wanted to be closer to her. Or at least, that had been the case before Rachel.

Now he'd seized the moment, using the whole wedding fiasco for his own benefit. Once Jack confirmed that Lexi had stepped in as his bride after Grace fled the church, Clint knew he'd use the opportunity to see Rachel again.

What a mess. He parked in front of her house, his gut clenching like he was about to ride a wild bronc.

He knocked on Rachel's door, hoping she'd be as eager to see him again as he was to see her. He'd skipped one of the art galleries where he hoped to show his photography and driven to Longmont, his heart racing as he found her street.

Meeting such a sexy woman while at his brother's wedding had been a stroke of luck. Bedding her had been amazing. Even talking to her had made him happy. Rachel didn't act like a suburban small-town school teacher. Her varied interests and viewpoints had kept him captivated, and that, even more than the sex, had him showing up on her front stoop. Well, okay, maybe sex and her personality were tied as far as motivators went.

He ran a hand through his short blond hair, yanked his shirt straight to remove wrinkles from his time in the car, and brushed at his jeans. Done fidgeting, he knocked.

Rachel pulled open the door. "Clint, what a surprise."

He grinned, unable to help it. Her tone came out flat, as though resigned to greeting him out of politeness, but her gaze ran over him like he was her favorite flavor of ice cream. "Rachel."

"What brings you here?"

She also sounded like she had a guess, and while sex placed high on his wish list, there was no sense in him coming off too eager. No woman wanted a man panting after her like a wolf over an orphaned calf.

Though he could be excused for panting when a woman looked like Rachel Marshall. Her slim body enticed a man. The memory of her plump breasts in his hands made his fingers tingle. Honey gold streaks mingled through her brown hair. Peachy tan cheeks and bright blue eyes drew him closer, and he longed to let his lips roam over her features. Her kisses had sent him spiraling into the stratosphere with need.

Except he hadn't driven all this way for sex, he reminded himself. He tipped his hat off. "I came here looking for your cousin."

Her mouth hung open for a second. "Why would you be looking for Lexi here? Why would you be looking for her at all?"

"Can I come inside?"

Rachel glanced behind her as though making sure none of her personal items sat in plain view, then peered at his convertible parked in the street. "I suppose you should. We wouldn't want the neighbors to talk."

Stepping over the threshold, he wondered why the neighbors mattered. She was a grown woman, unmarried. Her small foyer crowded the two of them together. He liked her nearness, liked the memories her presence evoked. Liked the idea of making more memories to carry back with him to L.A. This close, he wouldn't need to move to gather her into his arms and kiss her breathless.

Whoa. Slow and easy, he reminded himself. "How are you?"

"Fine. Would you like a drink? Tea or water is all I have."

"No thanks. I wondered if you knew where Grace might be."

She stared at him for a long moment. "Grace? Didn't she and Jack make it back to the ranch?"

"Not like you'd expect."

"What does that mean?" She placed a hand on her chest and her face flushed. Was she getting turned on?

That was probably just wishful thinking. He hadn't even made any advances yet, and he wasn't the kind of man women fainted over. Then she took a deep breath and reached out. For *him?* For the wall?

He grabbed her arm for support, feeling like an ass as he reviewed his words. "I'm sorry, Rachel. I should have thought how that sounded. I didn't mean to alarm you. Here." He led her five steps to the couch. "Sit down."

"I'm fine." She turned her face away while she regained her composure.

"Should I get you some water?" Dammit. He should be kicked in the pants for upsetting her.

"No, no. You just took me by surprise."

"I'm sorry. I'm sure Grace is fine. I didn't mean to scare you." He rubbed her arm. Comfort quickly turned to a caress as his heart drummed low and hard. Her soft skin under his hand brought memories of the night before, of her supple body responding to his. Those images had him shifting on the cushion, not uncouth enough to adjust himself right in front of her, despite his growing discomfort.

Rachel's gaze met his, and he read—*hoped* he read— desire.

Clint leaned toward her, his gut clenching with need. He couldn't help kissing her but kept it light and brief. "I didn't come here to have sex with you."

"Then don't." Her voice came out husky with both regret and invitation.

The invitation made his blood surge. "I don't seem to be able to stop myself."

Her hands against his chest halted his motion. "That's not exactly flattering. You're drawn to me against your will?"

"No, not at all. I'm very willing." He winked. "And able."

"Yet you didn't come for sex. You didn't come to see me at all, really."

"Rachel." He lifted her left hand to his lips and kissed it. She couldn't seriously believe that. "I drove three hundred miles out of my way to come here. I missed sunset in the canyon I had earmarked for the trip home, which would have made a stunning photo and pushed the art world into a bidding war for my work."

She smiled at his joke, and his tension eased as she relaxed.

"Sex with you," he continued in a low voice, intent on conveying his sincerity, "would have been a bonus, since I only needed to see your face to make the journey worthwhile."

She blinked.

He licked the crevices between her fingers, feeling her shiver as his tongue traced slow lines. Gaze on hers, he hoped to evoke memories of the night before when his tongue had made her shudder. When trust had formed and let them enjoy each other. When pleasure had made them one.

"Do you want something to drink?" she asked. "I just did the same nine hour drive. You must have been right behind me."

He smiled, thinking how he'd like to be right behind her. In bed. Her blush assured him she shared the image, but the hesitancy behind it clued him in not to belabor the point. "I'm good, thanks. I carry water all the time. Long habit from on the ranch." Sensing she needed a breather, he added, "I could use the restroom though."

Rachel led him down the hall then stepped back toward the kitchen. Why was she determined to serve him something? His mind dropped to the gutter, thinking of how she could serve him, and he hauled it back. Finishing quickly, he washed his hands and took a few extra seconds to rein in his eagerness. Her expression said yes and her body had softened toward his, but then she'd pulled away. He would finish whatever blasted drink she insisted on in record gulps and convince her to reenact the previous night's fun.

Smiling at the idea, Clint stepped into the kitchen to find her on her cell phone. Her gaze locked on his.

"Listen," she said into the phone, although she kept her gaze on him. "It's Rachel. I can't meet you for that movie, after all. You'll have to go without me. I'm going to be busy at home for a few hours. I'll call you later, when I'm free to talk."

They stared at each other as her thumb found the End button. She had freed up her night to be with him. Or to *be with* him? Had she just cleared her schedule for sex? If so, he'd make sure to show his appreciation. "Am I interrupting something?"

"Nothing that can't be rearranged."

He advanced with purpose then stopped as her words tripped him up. Had she had plans with a guy? Plans she'd finish later, after Clint headed home to California? He had no right to be annoyed at that. He should be grateful for the hours ahead. Still, it ticked him off to think he would be replaced so easily. To think of another man's hands on her. To think of another man in her bed.

His inner caveman raised his territorial head. "Let me rephrase. Did you have a date?"

"No. If I were seeing someone, I wouldn't have gone to bed with you last night. And I wouldn't be moments away from taking you to my bed today."

His smile spread slow and hot as his heart galloped. "That's a great answer."

He drew her to him, lips on hers as he tightened his arms. That crazy caveman needed reassurance. She gave it, her mouth opening for his invasion. Slow strokes now, deep and needy. Her moan set his heart to racing. Her fingers against his scalp pressed him closer, making him shiver with need. He pulled her into him, up on her toes, making her hang on to his shoulders.

He kissed across her soft cheek to her ear, gasping in air as she sucked at the cord in his neck. Thought fled as desire took over. Slowly, he slid his palm down her back to her rear and pressed her closer. Snuggled her pelvis against his erection so she could feel his need.

One of her hands ran across his chest. He returned the favor, only slower, with his fingertips at first, drawing circles, tracing his intention as he centered on her nipple. Then he cupped her breast, molded it. His head dipped.

Rachel leaned back, her hands coming up to deter him.

Clint froze, searching her expression. Thank God, stopping him altogether didn't seem to be her intention, not with those glazed eyes and that soft smile.

"Bedroom. Down the hall," she said.

His muscles bulged with renewed eagerness as heat cascaded through him. "Shall I carry you?"

"You'd have to catch me first." She took off, a step ahead of him as he followed her with a laugh.

A few days later, Rachel stared into the back room of her favorite restaurant where people milled in groups. Chairs anchored the strings of "Happy Birthday" balloons and silver balloons shaped into the number thirty. Ugh. She should have followed Clint back home to L.A.

"I didn't want a celebration." She tried not to grit her teeth as her dear cousin Grace, the runaway, pulled her into Vincenzo's restaurant. She didn't want to celebrate her thirtieth birthday. Age wasn't a big deal as far as numbers went, but this one marked another day alone.

Maybe next year she'd have someone special to celebrate with. Picturing the possibilities eased the tension from her shoulders.

"That's better," Grace said without moving her lips. "Now, smile and enjoy yourself."

Grace had been in her house on Sunday when Rachel arrived home from the wedding. Rachel had quickly surmised Lexi had been the bride whose wedding she herself had sniffled over, whose license she herself had witnessed. Whose reception she herself—and Clint—had skipped.

She didn't need Grace's reminder to smile now. The memory of her time with Clint accomplished that. When he'd shown up at her house late on Sunday afternoon, she'd looked around for anything Grace might have left in view when she left to fill her car with gas. Rachel had called Grace on her cell to warn her not to return for a few hours. Thankfully, Grace had understood her concocted story about a movie and stayed away until after Clint left.

Grace had thrown this party for Rachel on short notice—short, since Grace hadn't known she'd be in town. Rachel appreciated the bright balloons, cheery lights, and special touches Grace had added, staying clear of the black birthday most thirty-year-olds endured. Rachel couldn't imagine how Grace had spread the word and issued invitations within two days. Everyone was here, from her teaching colleagues to the administration to some of Rachel's neighbors.

And Henry Lanigan.

Her heart sank as she spotted her ex-boyfriend, but she kept a polite smile in place. He'd made it clear he wanted no part of her in the future. Their parting had not been amicable, but they still had to see each other every day at school, where they maintained a civil distance. A stiff and disapproving distance on his side, but at least he stayed quiet. She appreciated the small blessing.

He must have come to her party for appearance's sake. What would the other teachers and administration think if he were absent? They all knew she and Henry had dated and that their relationship had ended. No one knew why—at least she hoped not. She didn't want that news spread. Yet.

Rachel accepted a glass of white wine, drank to toasts to her health, chuckled along with jokes about her advanced age—some were even humorous—and snacked on the appetizers. She caught up with the few former students in attendance and thanked Anita, Paul, and Mike Thompson for helping Grace with decorations.

About half an hour passed before, from her peripheral vision, she noticed Henry slithering his way toward her. She snatched up a refill of wine. Even if Grace hadn't driven them to the party, Rachel would have taken the second glass for fortification. Henry no longer held any attraction for her, physically or otherwise, but his pointed remarks sometimes had barbs that cut.

"Happy birthday." Henry raised his glass to her.

She glanced around to check who stood near and discovered no one did. They drew glances from the guests, all eager for a bit of drama, but Rachel realized she'd edged away from his approach until she stood in a deserted corner of the room.

His flat brown eyes met hers behind his glasses. In the old days, he used to smile, showing off perfect and expensive orthodontia. His skin didn't gleam with a healthy tan nor glow a pasty white. He was ordinary. Neither tall nor short, handsome nor ugly, muscular nor flabby. Pretty unremarkable, now that she thought on it. His brown hair reflected no highlights, and his pleasant expression could be hiding any kind of thoughts. His neighbors would probably tell reporters he was a nice quiet man who would never (insert horrible crime here). The thought made her smile.

"Thank you," she said, raising her glass. "I'm surprised you came."

"We were friends, once upon a time, Rachel. More than friends."

"Before you learned I'm a—what was it you called me?— a morally corrupt woman?"

He stiffened, his gaze darting to check who might

overhear them as she had done. "I don't want to rehash that particular conversation. Not here."

"Not anywhere," Grace agreed. Her wine tasted warm and over-fermented. Or being near Henry soured everything around her, including her mood.

"There's no need to be nasty."

She choked as she tried to swallow. "Me? I seem to recall 'morally corrupt' was the nicest thing you called me."

His lips firmed. "You couldn't have expected me to approve, let alone participate in your plans."

"I thought we were friends, at the least. Closer than friends."

"We could have been."

She ignored his interruption. "Whether our relationship progressed or not, I mistook you for someone on my side. Who'd be invested in my plans, in my dreams for the future."

He tossed back his wine then scowled at her. "I said, there's no reason to rehash this."

"Then don't come to my birthday party and celebrate my next year, Henry, because I fully intend to make those dreams a reality. Without your help, it appears, and that is more than fine with me. I'd call it a near miss."

He glared. "Keep your voice down. And maybe stay off the booze."

Booze? She'd had not quite two glasses of wine over the

past hour, along with food. Who was he kidding?

She checked the crowd again, hoping to catch the eye of one of her friends who would come to her rescue. The principal huddled with other admins clear across the room, as though holding a meeting instead of attending a birthday party. The other guests steered clear of their area, too polite to intercept an SOS. Grace was having a terse conversation with Mike Thompson—what was that about? She'd have to ask Grace later. The point was, no one could overhear this conversation or save her from having to endure Henry's presence.

She could walk away, but she couldn't afford to make a scene. The man had ammunition and she didn't want to ignite any slow fuses. "I understand why you came, Henry. Now we've been seen being civil to each other in public, like we are at school. So you can go."

He squinted and leaned forward, peering into her face. "How much have you had to drink?"

That again? "I don't drink to excess, so you can drop that joke or whatever it is right now."

"Despite our break up, I'm concerned about you."

"Hah!" she barked, sounding as out of control as he accused. "You only care about yourself and what people think."

"Teachers should maintain a certain decorum. We're role

models. We cannot behave without thought to public opinion." His lip lifted in a sneer. "I hope you reconsider your foolhardy plans. I'd hate to have to mention your name to the school board if you follow through."

As she gaped, he walked past her toward the door. He was a total ass, but he did execute a great exit line.

Rachel bit her lip, glad no one had come over to soothe her and get the gossip. Henry had walked away from her, like he had in March when he broke off their relationship. They'd dated for almost a year, but something about him kept her from going to bed with him. Good instincts, she liked to think. When she broached the idea of him donating sperm, he'd left her. She'd been expecting him to walk away eventually, but she'd hoped against reason that Henry wouldn't be like her dad. That Henry would stand by her, maybe even get on board with her baby plans.

But no. He'd deserted her, and he'd departed with loud, nasty condemnation and a disgusted glare. At least her alcoholic, gambling-addicted father had snuck out of her and her mom's lives without a scene. And her step-father had packed up while she'd been at school and left after she'd gone to bed, giving her a goodnight kiss on the head that had been goodbye.

If Uncle Kevin hadn't been in her life as a role model, she'd believe all men were scum.

Not Clint, a little voice whispered in her head. But he'd been temporary, with no pressure on him. He'd probably never been in a serious, long-term relationship. Maybe *that* said something about him.

She didn't want her encounter with Henry to mar her memories of Clint. She'd had a lovely weekend, but now she'd returned to real life.

How long did she have to smile and make nice? She glanced at her watch and figured she could last another half an hour. Time to start the party winding down. Tomorrow was a school day, after all. The teachers all had homework to grade and end of year paperwork to tackle.

She grabbed an ice water to wash the encounter with Henry out of her mouth and approached a group to begin the goodbyes and nudge people toward the door.

Clint entered Rachel's number on his phone, amazed that his heart raced in anticipation of hearing her voice. The woman had gotten to him in their short time together. Her wicked dry humor. Her sharp intelligence. Her killer body. Maybe not in that order, especially at first. He'd enjoyed flirting with her during the rehearsal dinner. She hadn't taken him seriously. Not surprising, since in Little Tree, he was just Jack's younger brother. *The flighty one,* he was sure the townspeople said behind their hands. *Took off for* Los Angeles, *of all places.*

He smiled. No one was a hero in his hometown. In L.A., the big corporations courted him for his artistic eye, fast turnaround of projects, and flexibility when they wanted changes.

But at home? The townsfolk, and his brother for that matter, saw him as the kid that grew up semi-wild and fled at the first chance.

He paced his apartment as he waited for Rachel to answer her phone. When he heard her voice, his pulse raced and he took a breath. "Hi, it's Clint."

"I know." She paused and he wondered if she was pleased or not. "I saw the area code."

And she'd still picked up. Taking encouragement from that morsel made him feel pathetic.

"I didn't expect to hear from you," she said. "How's L.A.?"

"Lonely." The word escaped before he could stifle it. "How's Longmont?"

"Lonely."

It shouldn't have pleased him. What kind of jerk wanted her to be lonely? His kind, apparently.

"But I'm busy, busy, busy," she continued on an upbeat, "so I'm sure that'll change. I start next week teaching two summer classes. In one, the students are high achievers and will keep me on my toes. In the other, the students are struggling, so they're a challenge in a different way. One group wants to be there, the other not so much."

Her babbling gave him hope. He made her nervous, even at a distance. Something was happening between them other than sex. He twisted the phone away from his mouth for a second so she wouldn't hear his relieved and satisfied sigh. "Sounds like you have your hands full."

"Yes, I have to work on my lesson plans this week."

"I'd hoped you could come down here for a visit. A long visit." Like the rest of the summer, though he guessed her teaching made that improbable. "I didn't know you were working."

Rachel didn't say anything for a moment. He glanced around his living room, picturing her on his tan leather sofa with her feet up on the coffee table as they discussed where to go to dinner.

"Sorry," she said. "I can't because I am. Teaching."

"Yeah."

He didn't like the tension in her voice. Their relationship had been easy up to now. Meet, flirt, have sex, part, reunite, have sex. Seemed like a good pattern. Now Reality had shoved between them like a disapproving chaperone.

"I guess I could come up there for a long weekend over the Fourth of July." Clint cleared his throat. "If I'm invited. That feels like a long time from now, but I can be patient when

I want something. And I really want to be with you."

"Clint." His name squeezed through the earpiece, full of regret. "I can't."

He shook his head, denying her answer. "Can't?"

"I can't carry on an affair in the town where I teach. This isn't L.A. People would notice. I told you about the school board being ultra-conservative. What we had was lovely. I—"

Anger and a hint of panic turned his gut cold. "Don't talk about it in the past tense."

"It is, though. It has to be. Don't you see, this was just…a fling."

"No," he said with force. "It wasn't. Not to me."

"I had a great time with you. Can't we just leave it like that? Don't ruin the memory of it with an argument, please."

"Don't give me that, Rachel. It wasn't a fling. It was a beginning." He took a calming breath. "True, we haven't known each other long, but there's something between us."

She gave a laugh, which didn't fool him in the least. "Yeah, several thousand miles and a couple of mountain ranges."

"Not geography. Romance."

He heard her breath catch and felt like an idiot. Didn't she want more than sex?

"Not all romances end happily. I enjoyed knowing you, Clint."

"Wait," he insisted, fearing she'd hang up and that would be the end of their relationship.

"What?"

"Just tell me why you won't give us a chance. Did I do something wrong?" *Dammit.* He'd lose his Man Card if he didn't stop pleading.

"No, of course not. I made some goals before I met you. I still want to—need to—carry out the steps to achieve those goals. I don't mean to sound harsh, but I met you at a bad time."

"Maybe I could help with your goals, Rachel."

"I wouldn't ask you to. Because…"

Her hesitations were killing him. Offering him hope, snatching it away when she spoke. Maybe this time, she'd relent. He could fly down and—

"I'm going to have a baby."

He staggered and reached for the chair behind him, falling into it.

Rachel didn't say more after that pronouncement. Had she hung up or had he gone deaf with shock? The hum of his a/c unit reassured him only the call had ended, not his whole existence.

A baby. How could she know already? They'd just had sex. There hadn't been time.

His mind cleared as though he'd been slapped upside the

head by Uncle Crusty. Of course. The baby wasn't his. He'd gone stupid there for a minute.

A baby. Had she known before, at the wedding, while they were together? He'd used a condom, as always, but it obviously hadn't been necessary for birth control.

His gut went hollow.

A baby. Rachel had someone else in her life.

He was surprised to care this much after such a short acquaintance. Why couldn't he shrug it off? Admit she had her own plans and only considered him...wild oats? Hopefully, she'd smile fondly about her last crazy weekend with a stranger and then continue her plans with the baby daddy.

No. That just didn't feel true, didn't seem like what Rachel would do. Granted, Clint hadn't known her long, but he couldn't believe she'd sleep with him under those circumstances, with another guy in the wings and a baby in her future. And she'd assured him at her house that she didn't have a guy in her life.

He took a breath and let it out on a jagged laugh. What the hell was he going to do now? He ran a hand over his face, trying to focus. His brain said, *Forget her.* She had her future mapped out without him in it. She'd raise her baby and be an excellent mom. Without him or his assistance.

Call it a narrow escape. Have a beer. Have a couple dozen *beers and toast your freedom.* That sounded about right.

Clint exhaled as he adjusted to Rachel's news and how it changed his plans. In a minute, he'd head to the kitchen and find the first of those celebratory beers.

Once he could trust his legs to work.

CHAPTER FOUR

"You're having a baby?"

Rachel swung around, tears on her cheeks, a hand to her breastbone in surprise. "Oh, crap, Grace. I didn't know you were home."

Grace walked over and pulled Rachel into a hug. "Are you happy about it? Because you don't look happy."

Rachel shook her head. "I'm very happy."

They sat on the couch while she explained about saving up for artificial insemination, trying to plan how to get pregnant at the end of this school term in order to stretch out her time with her baby over the next summer break. "I have the money saved. I want a child. It's easier and less expensive to get pregnant than to adopt."

Grace nodded. "What about the future? It'll be harder to date. It'll be harder to find a man who wants a ready-made family."

Rachel's enthusiasm dimmed at the reminder. She'd had her last hurrah with Clint, knowing the difficulties ahead. If she ever met a man who would support her decisions, who would stay around, and who, most importantly, wouldn't be like her father, she believed he would also accept her child. But she wasn't holding her breath. "It's time to start living the life I want."

Grace squeezed Rachel's fingers, lending her support. "And single motherhood is the life you want?"

Rachel stood, paced away, then turned to face her cousin. "No, of course not. I'd like to be in love. I'd like a man to love me forever. Someone to build a family with. But that guy isn't here." She gestured to the room before letting her arm fall against her thigh. From her past experiences with her dad, with Henry and other men she'd dated, she doubted such a man existed. "I can't wait forever for Prince Charming to come along."

She explained about the babysitter she had in mind, the nanny companies she'd already started interviewing. Grace shook her head, looking impressed with all her planning. "Whatever I'm doing next year, I promise you at least a week of help."

Rachel had to laugh at the determination on her cousin's face—and the panic in her eyes. "You look even more terrified than I am."

"A little bit. What's the first step?"

Rachel burst with laughter. "Well, that'll be up to the

sperm. I'll let you know when I need you."

She couldn't help but hug Grace. Talking out the plan with someone made it feel less crazy. When she'd told Henry, he had been scathing. That had been a narrow escape, in her view. If he was that reluctant to be a sperm donor, he'd have made a terrible father. Having her cousin's support meant everything. Grace and Lexi had been her summer sisters, easing Rachel's loneliness of being an only child. As they grew older, they'd stayed close between visits as well, and were always there for each other to listen, commiserate and advise.

Rachel made a decision on the spot. Once this baby was born, she would start saving for the next insemination. She wanted her child to have siblings.

Clint pounded on Rachel's front door Friday night, sweating so hard he feared he'd need another shirt. That feeling of a narrow escape had never materialized and he'd never had beers to celebrate. He'd only felt confused and angry, and *yes, dammit, hurt.*

"Clint," Rachel said in a voice loud enough to carry to the neighbors. "This is quite a surprise."

"Is it?" Clint couldn't believe she would say such a thing. He ran his gaze over her, gauging her health. She didn't look pregnant. "You tell me you're having a baby but you don't expect me to show up? What kind of asshole do you think I am?"

"I don't think you're any kind of an asshole."

He stared, disbelieving. "You're joking at a time like this?"

"No better time."

A sound in the kitchen had him looking that way. "Do you have company?"

"No, no. Here, come sit." Rachel took his hands and led him to the couch where she pulled him to sit facing her. Her gaze strayed to the window behind him. "I'm sorry you came all this way."

He'd practiced his speech on the plane, though the words never did fall into place as he'd have liked. He squeezed her hands. "I don't want you to have to go through this alone, Rachel. You don't have to."

Touched, she could barely find her breath. "Oh my gosh. Clint, that's so nice. Thank you. Having friends will help."

"I'm pleased you consider me a friend. I hope you think of me as a close friend. I'd like to be more."

Her eyes went wide as she no doubt guessed his intention.

"I came here to say—"

"Clint—"

"No, let me finish while I can. I want to help you raise this baby." There. He would have let out a relieved sigh on finishing, but his breath stayed trapped in his lungs, awaiting her answer.

"Oh, Clint, that's so sweet." Tears glistened in her eyes. "Thank you. I'll never forget that you offered, but it isn't necessary."

His gut sank. She had a guy already in her life. Of course, he knew a man figured in there somewhere—she *was* pregnant after all. But she must have gotten back together with the jerk. Clint couldn't believe his disappointment. He should wish her well and get the hell out of Dodge, congratulating himself on that narrow escape.

And he would, as soon as he made sure she was with the right guy. "Let's clear this up, starting with the basics. Where's the baby's father?"

At least that was the basic question as far as Clint was concerned. The jerk better be standing by her.

"I don't know yet."

"Is he worthy of you? And why—?" He stopped, confused. "What?"

She laughed. *Laughed?* Did pregnancy hormones make a woman crazy?

"I'm not pregnant yet, but I am *going to* have a baby, as I told you. That's my plan."

Clint slumped against the sofa. *Not pregnant* was all he heard. Over and over, like the song "It's a Small World" replaying in his head but a million times more welcome. "Not pregnant?"

She shook her head. "Not yet, but I'm hoping to be by the end of the summer."

If she planned to get pregnant, why had they used a condom when they'd been together? Didn't that defeat the purpose? He always used a condom, but a clever woman could have found a way. Saved the condom, run to the bathroom, inserted it inside out? The image made him grimace. She wouldn't have done that, nor did he recall her jumping from the bed. Had it been the wrong time of the month for her to conceive? Clint didn't really know much about baby-making. He'd spent the last decade trying to prevent that from happening.

The gears tumbled until they fell into place. Artificial insemination. Baby-making from a tube. He couldn't decide if he was relieved she didn't have a man or annoyed she didn't consider one necessary. "*In vitro*?"

She nodded.

"Why do you want to do that? Do you...?" He waved a hand toward her abdomen, thinking of Sheryl. "Have some problem conceiving?"

"No. I mean, I haven't tried to conceive yet, but I don't think so."

"Then why this way? Why not find a guy, get married, do it the nor—" He stopped when her lovely blue eyes narrowed.

"Conventional way?"

"I want a child now. My biological clock is ticking."

He snorted before he could stop himself. Sheryl had said the same about her twenty-two-year-old clock. Then she'd purposely gotten knocked up by some random guy whose name she didn't even remember. The idea of it happening again, to Rachel, turned his gut to ice. "It's not like you're old, Rachel."

"I just turned thirty."

"Oh, well, then, I take it back. How will you ever be able to raise a child at your advanced age?"

"Ha, ha. A husband would be great, but there's no guarantee I'll find a man I love and like enough to marry any time soon. Then, of course, there's the matter of could we conceive right away or would he even want to."

"Okay, I get that. It might take two years or six or more. But you're still young."

"And I want to be a new mother while I'm young. Who knows, I might want more than one child."

The blood ran from his face as cold sweat broke out on his skin. Another one? "Let's just concentrate on this first baby, okay? Are you prepared?"

"I'll never have enough money saved for a child—I've heard no one does, but I have enough to start."

"That's another thing. It costs a lot to have a fake donor,

doesn't it?"

"Sperm comes from a real donor," she said with studied patience, "but yes, it's a costly procedure."

"You've thought out an answer to every argument."

"Not even close, but I have thought about this, Clint. For a long time. I don't know if a man could even comprehend what I'm going through." She looked at him, beseeching his understanding. "My arms feel empty."

The words pierced his heart, and he took a deep breath. He hadn't stepped up last time, with Sheryl and that had been a tragic disaster. He'd declared himself Rachel's friend. Time to prove it. "How can I help?"

Those words hung between them. He thought of the most obvious way, though that was far from what he meant. He tried to suppress a grin, right up until he saw her eyes light with laughter.

"Hey," he said, straight-faced. "Great idea brewing over here. I know exactly what I can do."

"No." But she was laughing.

"Hear me out." He started to list this idea. "I'm cheap— well, affordable. I only need to be fed. And I'm good at the sex part."

"Too true."

"I'm warmer and friendlier than a tube."

"Injection syringe."

He flinched. "Even worse."

"I appreciate your offer, but think about it, Clint. Do you really believe you'd be able to deal with knowing you have a child but not ever seeing him or her?"

That sounded like a crappy future. Still, every problem had a work-around, and his creative brain started brewing solutions. "Who says that's how it would happen?"

"I do." Her chin almost jutted out with the declaration. "I'm not looking to rope a guy into fatherhood. That's the beauty of this donor process."

"Because Man-in-a-Tube doesn't demand visitation rights?"

"Something like that. I don't owe him anything, either."

"Why raise the baby alone when I'm offering to help?"

"We're not in love, Clint. We're not a couple."

"I remember coupling with you."

"Sex does not make a relationship."

"So we start one. We like each other. We're good in bed."

"You live in California," she interrupted.

"I can move. I'm ready to try my hand at photography full-time."

"Clint."

"I was just talking to Grace about it this past week."

"How? Oh, right. Before the wedding."

"Yeah, I thought she'd be all wrapped up in wedding

plans, but it wasn't as hard as I'd thought it would be to get her to talk art. You should take that as a warning, I guess. Artists are absorbed in their work."

"Then you'd be a terrible candidate."

"Not at all." He took her hands again. "I could carry the baby in a pack and we'd hike everywhere together."

She looked horrified. "Because *that* sounds safe."

He gave her a persuasive smile. "You know I'd be careful. I'd be good for the baby, taking it out for fresh air."

"You missed the part about us not being a couple."

"Right. I'll move here and we'll work on conceiving. That ought to give us time to work out who sleeps on which side of the bed."

Her hand pressed against her chest. "You're going to live with me?"

Clint feared that quiver in her voice was horror instead of the hoped-for excitement. She looked like her heart might burst from her chest. Again, not with eagerness to be with him, either.

"It's the best way to conceive. Lots of time together to—" He waggled his brows. "Do the deed."

She blushed. *Blushed.* He wanted to crow with relief. Maybe excitement mixed in there somewhere for her.

"You have a job."

"I'll switch positions." It was too soon to tell her more.

Would she consider him a good prospect if she knew he planned to quit his job and take up photography full time? "If my employers won't cooperate with me working off-site, I'll find a company that will. You may not realize this, but I'm very good at what I do."

She deflated like a sailboat with no wind. "I can't believe you'd want to raise a child with me. I gave up on the thought of involving a guy."

"I have some savings, Rachel. You're not the only one who's been thinking of making life changes." Of course, he'd been saving to go back home to Little Tree, but hey. Plans change.

"Why would you want to?"

Clint didn't want to ask himself that question, let alone answer it. Because he didn't have an answer other than guilt over Sheryl. He only knew he couldn't let Rachel go through this alone. "Wouldn't you rather know your baby came from a clean bloodline? The Walkers are good stock."

"I don't doubt that. And it's not the point."

"The point is, I'm willing to help you conceive. Willing and able." He smiled. "And did I mention willing?"

A slight smile twitched at her mouth. "I believe so. And I'd be tempted to take you up on it if it was only for your sperm."

"That's so romantic."

"That's the real point, isn't it, Clint? We're not romantic. We've had sex. Good sex. A lot of sex."

"Not that much," he objected.

"Not enough."

All the blood rushed out of his face again, but straight to his groin this time.

"But," she continued before he could follow up on her comment, "enough to know I'd like to have more. And I'd like to have your genes for my baby. So I'm almost tempted."

His heart raced. "What can I say to convince you? We could go practice."

She laughed at his hopeful expression. "We could, and we might. You're like a donut. I shouldn't have you, but I can't resist."

"A donut." She meant it as a compliment, but shouldn't he be something a lot more manly, like a steak? A juicy rib-eye?

"But having sex with you doesn't solve the problem."

"It might solve my current problem."

She rubbed his thigh, adding to the problem. "Concentrate."

"Then stop doing that."

Unfortunately, she took his suggestion. "Be honest. Do you seriously want to have a baby, Clint?"

He studied her and considered. A baby. A child. Forever.

With Rachel. "I flew here on the first plane I could manage. I had the entire flight to weigh options. I could have turned around without you ever knowing."

She swallowed. "You coming here means so much."

"When I thought you were already pregnant with another man's baby, I offered to help you raise the child. Be in its life. Be in your life."

"But I'm not pregnant. You're off the hook."

"Tell me you'd rather have an unknown donor." He let that sink in for a moment. "That you'd rather have a science experiment rather than me as the child's donor."

"I don't want to complicate your life, Clint."

"If I donated sperm, would you want to use it?"

"Yes. Absolutely. That's not the question."

"Then let me donate sperm. A little more personally." He grinned, warming to the idea. The intimacy of giving her a baby sent warmth over his skin. Candles, soft music. Every thrust a prelude, every burst of ejaculate a possible conception. If asked, he'd never have imagined this response to getting a woman pregnant. Especially a woman not his wife. He hadn't been tempted with Sheryl—and he'd planned to propose to her. Maybe it was guilt prodding him or maybe it was just the right time now. "Let me do this for you. I'd be honored, as a friend, to give you what you long for."

She wet her lips. "And after?"

"We'd do it again."

Rachel swatted his arm with the back of her hand, a slight chuckle escaping. "You know what I mean."

He pictured Sheryl lying in her bed in the hospital after the accident. Now unable to have a baby. With a permanent limp and a drug addiction. He didn't blame himself for her condition. She'd made her own decisions, her own mistakes. But he'd played a part. Made bad decisions himself.

His mind cleared and he saw the path before him laid out straight and true. He only knew this felt right. "After, I could move to town, though I'd prefer to move in with you. Be the male role model, though I'd prefer to be the daddy."

"Would you? Would you really?"

"I would."

She stared at him, thinking hard. "And us?"

"If we live together before the baby is born, we'd know if we worked as a couple. If not, I'd move out, but stay in town for the kid. We'd be friends, united by our child."

"It sounds so civilized when you say it."

"I was raised a cowboy, I live in L.A., and I grew up wanting to be a landscape photographer. Don't expect a stereotype from me." Clint clapped his hands together, ending the intense moment. "So, should I call my boss and negotiate a new position with the company?"

"The baby won't even be born until next year."

"Perfect. I'll give them my nine months' notice at work."

"Clint, don't do anything hasty. Let's think about this, at least for a couple of days."

He kissed her, lightly, as a friend would. No tongue. "I think what you need is for me to audition."

"I don't have that short of a memory."

"Let's give that baby-making a practice run. Then if you go for the donor thing, you'll have a head start."

"You are persuasive." She ran a hand up his arm, over his shoulder, cupped his chin.

"Hey," Clint called from the bedroom doorway an hour later as he noticed her set her cell phone on the nightstand. "You don't have Man-in-a-Tube on speed dial, do you?"

"I'll put your name in my Contacts, if you'd like." She winked. "Right next to his."

"Well, that's something, I suppose." He set the tray of ham sandwiches on her lap. The tall glass of milk and a bottle of beer wobbled as she adjusted her position.

"That beer for me?"

"No way, little mama. You need to build up your bones." He made a face. "Or something. I don't know much about human conception, but I'll read up."

Her expression closed. "Clint, don't get ahead of yourself. I haven't made a decision yet. I'm not even sure I'm going to agree to you being the donor."

"Hold your milk."

Her face crumpled into confusion. "Is that some weird ranch expression?"

He chuckled and picked up the beer. "I'm getting in beside you and I don't want to spill your drink."

"Oh."

He maneuvered with the bottle in one hand and settled in against the headboard. Tapping his bottle to her glass, he said, "Let's eat."

They took their time, the silence a welcome buffer to the tension he felt and suspected she felt as well. He'd been too keyed up to eat dinner on the plane. He'd need strength for their conversation, especially if she continued to object to his involvement. In his mind, this was a done deal. A tube was probably fine for a woman without options, but that wasn't Rachel. Not anymore.

She took his empty plate and bottle and set it with hers on the tray, then moved the tray to the floor outside the door. Thankfully, she climbed back in beside him.

He slid down in the bed.

She pursed her lips. "Don't you think we should talk some more?"

He shook his head, letting a naughty smile form on his face. She wasn't ready to concede, wasn't ready to let him "sacrifice" for her. And frankly, he shied away from examining how crazy this plan was. He would be her sperm donor. Hopefully, they'd get along in the coming months and he'd become her friend as well as her partner in the pregnancy. If all the gods smiled upon them, he'd be a father by next year. And he'd either live with Rachel or nearby, providing support and watching his child grow. Being part of its life.

Excitement built in his chest like he'd just ridden a wild bull for eight seconds. And he felt just as crazy. And just as sure of his course.

Rachel turned off the bedside lamp and slid down over him. Her silky hair brushed his face and chest, and his body responded to the caress. He pulled her closer with a gentle hand on her shoulder.

"No condom this time," he said just before their lips met.

Her lips curved into a smile against his mouth.

Was that a yes? His every cell waited for the answer.

"Yes."

Clint gripped the phone, all awareness of his office dissipating like steam from his coffee cup as he recognized Rachel's voice. Then the word registered—and the meaning behind it. "What? Really?"

"Yes."

"Say it."

Rachel inhaled. "I want you to be my baby's father. There's no one else I want."

"Holy hell, Rachel. You won't be sorry."

"I'm not. I won't be." She giggled through the line, lighthearted or light-headed or both. "I canceled my appointment at the fertility clinic. You're definitely much more enticing than an injection syringe."

"Gee, thanks." He laughed as blood raced through his veins. It wasn't only the prospect of having sex that thrilled him, though the anticipation factored in. He was going to be a dad. By this time next year, he'd have a little boy or girl in his arms.

Clint remembered Rachel saying her arms were empty. He didn't quite feel that. Just pride. Excitement. Expectation. Waiting would kill him. Already his chest had expanded to near bursting. She had to get pregnant now. Soon. "When?"

"When what?"

"When are you...you know, fertile?"

This time she laughed. "Oh, my God. I can't believe I'm going to have to tell you that kind of stuff."

"We're in this together."

"I know. All the way."

He relaxed at the assurance. "So?"

"I'll text you."

"Coward." The word echoed in the room like an

endearment. The woman made him smile. She made his heart swell and pound and race and explode. God, if any of his friends knew he acted this stupid, almost as *giddy* as a schoolgirl, over getting a woman pregnant, he'd definitely have to turn in his Man Card.

Helping Rachel conceive gave him the push to follow his own dreams. She knew he wanted to quit his job and try to support himself—and them—on his photography, and she still approved of his being in her life and in her child's life. In *their* child's life.

He would have agreed to sperm donation and found a way to live with not raising his kid. Somehow, some way, for Rachel, he would have made the adjustment. To think of the baby as not his. But he didn't have to, due to her generosity and belief in him.

She wanted him to share her life and child. Talk about taking a chance on a guy. He calmed, going from exuberation to warm gratitude in a flash. "Thank you, Rachel."

"Thank *me?* You've got that backward, cowboy."

He wouldn't argue the point. "I've got vacation saved. Just say when."

"The middle of the month is my next fertile time." She cleared her throat, probably not comfortable discussing such intimate details with him. They'd both have to get used to it. "Will that be a problem?"

"I'll make it work."

"I've calculated the dates several times on my calendar," she continued. "I want to conceive now so I have the baby in April. Then my eight weeks of maternity leave will flow into the summer break and I'll get four months home with the baby."

He counted it out on his fingers. "Wouldn't a July conception bring the baby at the beginning of April?"

"The baby's approximate due date is nine months and seven days after the start of a woman's, uh, cycle. It actually takes forty weeks, or really two hundred and forty days, to be considered full term. Getting pregnant in mid-July means the baby comes in mid- to late April. I can take the week off to rest and prepare. Or in case the baby comes early. Perfect timing."

"Well then, we better get started."

She laughed, joy and excitement ringing through the airwaves. "Two weeks. I can't believe it. In two weeks, I could be pregnant. Thank you. So so much."

"My pleasure." He grinned. "Definitely."

"Will you be able to get away? Get a flight?"

"I'll be there, don't worry."

"With bells on?"

He shook his head, though she couldn't see him. "With nothing on."

She gasped out a laugh as she disconnected. Clint looked

around him and realized he stood in his office grinning like an idiot. He had things to do, clients to please, projects to finish.

Because he was going to need a few days off work.

CHAPTER FIVE

July

Rachel met him on her porch Friday night, throwing open the door and running out. Her enthusiastic greeting made his heart soar. Clint swept her into his arms, twirling her around. Both laughed, giddy and stupid. Definitely going to have to turn in his Man Card. He set her on her feet, making sure she had her balance before releasing his hold. "Let's go inside."

He grabbed his overnight bag and stepped into the house. "I left work a little early to make my flight. I couldn't wait— and not just for sex. Although…" He smiled.

"Was that okay with your boss?"

Clint shrugged. "I'm planning to leave my job anyway. If he doesn't like it, I'm not going to cry over it."

Her hand flattened on her chest, a move he'd already noted meant either excitement or dismay. "Maybe you should wait on that."

His gut tightened. Dismay then. "I haven't made any permanent moves yet in that area. I did put out some feelers to other companies though." He peered at her expression but couldn't read her. They'd talked about this, hadn't they? For the life of him, he couldn't remember what she'd said about him moving to Colorado or moving in with her. "They seemed interested in me freelancing for them. I made it clear I'm still in the planning stage."

He tacked that on in hopes of calming her while he got his bearings. "I'll take my bag up. Your room or a guest room?"

She snapped out of it and stared at him, looking as uncertain as he felt. "There's a guest room and bath across from mine. I cleaned it today, as a matter of fact. Fresh sheets and all."

He dropped his bag and took her by the arms. "I'm not going to need fresh sheets unless you toss me out of your bed. Are you going to do that?"

She shook her head with a slight, relieved smile. "Unlikely."

He blew out a breath and kissed her forehead. "Okay then."

Letting go of her, he found his own arms grasped.

Rachel blinked her eyelashes flirtatiously, a thing that always made him laugh. "Are you in a hurry to unpack, cowboy?"

Hell, he didn't even have to get out a condom. "Why, yes, ma'am, I am in a hurry." He swept her into his arms and started up the stairs. She laughed and tried to protest, but he shook his head. "There's something I've been wanting to do for a few weeks now, and daylight's burning."

They spent a leisurely morning in bed, awake, before enjoying a breakfast of eggs and bacon. The man could eat. While a scrambled egg on toast would have filled her, Rachel watched as he scooped three eggs and half a pound of bacon on his plate. So much for BLTs and midnight snacks. She had to smile though. She could get used to feeding a man his breakfast. This man, anyway.

But she couldn't get too attached. Who knew how long he'd be around when the fun ended and reality set in? She'd told Grace she had a donor but hadn't mentioned Clint's name. If he disappeared between conception and birth, she didn't want any hard feelings between the families. Speaking of which...

She cleared the table, trying to find the right words. Clint helped her load the dishwasher before they moved to the couch. He looked ready for a snuggle, and maybe more, but nerves kept her from sitting right beside him. She had too much on her mind to keep it all in.

"I thought you'd be in Little Tree this weekend. I'm glad you're here, of course, for the baby making." She shrugged, feeling awkward and embarrassed. "And just to see you. I'm surprised though, and honored, that you chose to come here. What did you tell Jack?"

He shook his head as though to clear it. "What did I tell Jack about what? About this? About us?"

She nodded, finding it hard to swallow. Their first test. What would their families say?

"I didn't tell him anything. It's none of his business." Clint rocked his head side to side in consideration. "I mean, not yet. Not until I can tell him he's going to be an uncle. It's a little early." His quick smile faded. "Why? Did you want me to tell him what we're doing?"

She opened her mouth and closed it. That was a lot to respond to. "Well, first off, and most importantly" —she took a breath— "I thought you'd be at the wedding."

"What wedding?"

She froze. Oh boy. "Jack and Lexi are getting married today."

His jaw dropped and his eyes bugged out. She bit her lip to keep from chuckling, not sure he'd appreciate her laughing at his expense.

"What!"

"Re-married, I should say. Lexi was the bride at the ceremony we witnessed."

Clint's mouth closed and he shook his head. "I knew that, about the first wedding. That's why I came looking for

Grace."

Rachel winced guiltily. Grace was yet another thing to discuss.

"Let me rephrase," Clint said. "I used looking for Grace as the excuse to be with you again."

He'd read her reaction as hurt feelings. She had to come clean, and the sooner the better. "I have something to confess."

Clint tensed, and she could imagine the thousand things running through his mind.

"Grace has been here at my house the whole time. This is where she ran to when she left the church last month."

"You're kidding."

She shook her head. "Remind me not to send you looking for anything hard to find, like diapers."

Clint laughed. "I'm pretty good at finding calves lost in gullies. I would have found Grace if I'd looked harder. Somehow I got sidetracked from my mission."

"In the most delightful way."

"And I learned you're good at hiding things." He sobered as their gazes met.

Rachel reached over and put her hand on his. "Your brother is married to my cousin. There's no way I could have a baby and you wouldn't find out about it. Plus, you have access to the information by asking Jack, Lexi or Grace. Although I hope you don't believe I would ever do that to you."

He nodded his acceptance. "Seems my big brother thinks he can get away with something without my knowing it though. And a wedding, at that. I need to call him."

"Of course."

Rachel waited while Clint went outside to make the phone call. The other questions he posed ran through her mind. Did she want him to tell Jack, and thereby, her family? Grace knew the baby part, but not the identification of the donor. How would Jack take that news? Lexi would probably stand by Rachel, whatever she did. Would Uncle Kevin be disappointed or elated? His opinion mattered more than anyone's. He'd filled in for his brother as her father figure even when her dad was alive. He'd been the only constant male in her universe.

Clint walked in and closed the door behind him, leaning on it as he shook his head. "They're all crazy."

"Who?"

"Everyone in Little Tree. All our relatives, at least."

"What's going on?"

Clint came and sat beside her on the couch. "There's a wedding today, as you said. Lexi and Jack are renewing their vows to eliminate any legal problems regarding the first ceremony."

"And because they love each other?" she asked with hope.

"I think so. I mean, yeah. Jack said he did."

"You asked him that?"

"Sure. I had to be certain he wanted this wedding. I had an inkling after the first wedding that something was weird between him and Lexi, once I figured out he'd married Lexi." He ducked his head. "I, uh, wasn't happy about the switch and might have said a few rude things about her."

"Understandable." She'd give him this one. As much as she loved her cousins, he loved his brother. They both had strong family ties. It was one of the many things she liked about Clint.

"Right." He blew out a breath. "Jack defended her. Strongly. That got me to remembering how peculiar he was when he thought I was flirting with Lexi at the rehearsal."

She raised a brow, hiding her amusement.

"Not with anything behind it. I mean, we were joking around. Neither Lexi or I ever had any feelings of that sort. We're like friends or nearly-siblings."

She delighted in watching him sweat, but she let him off the hook. "I believe you."

"Good. Anyway, Jack and Lexi wanted to keep this ceremony small since they've had the big church wedding, and they didn't want to draw attention."

A worry niggled at Rachel. "You said something about legal issues. What's that about?"

"I think it's Jack being super-protective, but the idea came up that she'd committed fraud. I don't think Lexi did anything intentionally," he rushed on when Rachel frowned, "but even accidentally going through with the ceremony, if such a thing is possible, might have looked fishy to a lawyer. And she did sign the marriage license, knowing it wasn't issued to her."

"I hadn't thought of her being in trouble."

"Like I said, it probably wouldn't have been an issue, but with Crusty leaving the land to Jack and Grace Walker, it got sticky." He brightened, laughter on his face. "And it gets crazier."

"How could it possibly?"

"Grace is there."

"I know. She left here to mend fences."

"Wow, you really can keep a secret. Anyway," he seemed to shake it off, "she served as Lexi's witness today."

Now Rachel's jaw dropped. "You're kidding. I thought she meant to crawl home begging for forgiveness."

"Did you know she took a new boyfriend with her?"

"Well...*boyfriend* might be overstating their relationship. She met a friend of mine while she was here. The first day, as I understand it. Things had been tense between them, but when he offered to go with her to help her drive and keep her safe on the road... I guess I wasn't paying much attention to Grace this month. I've been selfishly thinking about you and the baby."

"Can't say I disapprove of that."

"Grace." Rachel shook her head. Then she gave a laugh. "You're right. They're all crazy. Makes what we're doing seem almost logical."

"Speaking of crazy." Clint wiped his palms on his jeans. "I'd like to take you on a date. Would you go out to dinner with me tonight?"

A thrill started in her chest and spread throughout her body, warm and tingly. The suggestion was unexpected but... "Why would that be crazy?"

He shrugged. "We're already having sex. I feel like we missed some steps."

"That would be true," she said, testing each word before speaking, "if we were a normal couple with a normal relationship."

"Well, we're not abnormal."

"You know what I mean."

"Does that mean you don't want to go to dinner with me?"

So now here she stood, holding clothes up to her body as though she didn't know what she looked like in each outfit already. The LBD might look like she had expectations, so she cast it aside. Surely he didn't mean to go anywhere dressy, but then, it *was* their first date. Rachel tried to suppress the tingle that persisted in running through her, despite all her rational reminders to herself. Not the red spaghetti strap dress. *Too flimsy*. Theirs was not a romantic relationship, despite the sex and sizzle. Hmm. She held up the red again. It wouldn't hurt to try to entice him. Just because sex was a foregone conclusion didn't mean she could phone it in.

But again, she didn't want him thinking she expected more. Maybe the navy suit she wore to administrative meetings? No. Their relationship wasn't *business,* and they were more than casual friends. She'd be extremely interested in him if she weren't fixated on this baby plan—and if she wanted to set herself up for more heartache when he left. Maybe the blue off-the-shoulder gypsy top with the swirly rainbow skirt. Fun and young. *Too young?*

She groaned. Overthinking it would make her crazy. Rachel grabbed up the blue blouse. Decision made. She showered and put her hair up, sticking bobby pins all over to leave her hair fluffier than the bun she usually wore. With the lower neckline and her hair up, she felt half-naked. Instead of being self-conscious, it made her smile, imagining Clint's reaction. She usually only dressed for her own pleasure and comfort. Dressing for Clint, choosing her underthings with his reaction in mind, made each choice an act of deliberate seduction.

When she saw him waiting for her at the bottom of the stairs and noticed his reaction to her outfit, she was glad she'd taken the time and fussed a little.

"You look amazing."

His eyes darkened and his sexy little smile told her his thoughts, but she appreciated the words. She paused two steps from the bottom and deliberately ran her gaze over him. He wore gray slacks and an indigo dress shirt that sparked the green in his eyes. "You clean up pretty well yourself."

She sauntered—and hoped she didn't look ridiculous—down the remaining steps and leaned into him. Standing on the bottom stair, she matched him in height. Their lips aligned and her arms around his neck were more embrace than support. The kiss lingered, soft, without an agenda as they had all night to explore and enjoy each other.

"Hi." Clint's smile lit her through and through.

"Hi." Rachel nuzzled the tender area on his neck right below his ear. "Want to go out and eat or..." She ran her tongue up the cord of his neck to his earlobe. "Go out later?"

He shuddered and tightened his hands around her waist. Unfortunately, he set her away from him. "You're trouble. Here I am, trying to be a gentleman, and you're undermining my efforts."

"Did I say you had to be a gentleman?"

"Thankfully, no." He grinned. "But I want to be. For you. Get your purse and let's go before I let you change my mind."

She did as he requested, smiling to herself. She loved being able to seduce him, despite his resistance—although he wasn't fighting very hard. Since he didn't know the area, she'd thought of a few restaurants to go to for dinner, depending on his food preferences. "Do you have a place in mind?"

"I did a few searches while waiting for you to dress." He held open the door and waited while she locked it behind them. Taking her elbow, he escorted her to his car and opened the door for her.

His manners made her heart pitter-pat as he waited for her to gather her flowing flowered skirt before closing the door. She hadn't missed him eyeing her legs. Other parts of her pitter-patted in anticipation.

After discussing the options, Clint drove them to Rachel's favorite Mexican restaurant. "There are many good ones in the area," she said, "but this is the most authentic. Or so my friend Mike says."

"Mike?"

"I taught his sister and tutored both her and their brother. Great family." She slid Clint a look and noticed his determined lack of expression. Interesting. "He drove to Little Tree with Grace yesterday for Lexi and Jack's wedding."

"Oh." He didn't say more, but his jaw relaxed.

Rachel smiled.

On the way to the restaurant, they talked about music. Learning Clint enjoyed multiple genres, she said, "I need to take you to Red Rocks for a concert."

"What concert?"

"Doesn't matter. It's the venue that's outstanding. It's built into the hillside, just west of Denver. Everything sounds good there."

"I've heard of it," he said. "Let me know which concert you want to see and I'll fly in."

Rachel described some of her favorite performances at the amphitheater, and sooner than she knew it, they had arrived. Fortunately, they had only a short wait while a table was cleaned, and the owners' five-year-old son regaled them with knock-knock jokes during that time. His older sister came and shooed him off. "Sorry about that. He thinks he works here, but he's only here because the babysitter is running late."

Rachel smiled. "It's fine. I like kids."

"She really does." Clint had a twinkle in his eye that earned him a swat on the arm as soon as the server turned her back. "Ow."

"Behave."

He leaned in behind her. "That's not what you said this morning. Or last night. Or—"

"Hush." Rachel tried not to giggle, but her cheeks flamed

with embarrassment. "What if someone overhears you?"

"They'd be jealous."

Settled at their table, Clint looked around. She hoped he approved. It was a cute place with carved wood and boldly painted furnishings. Fake plants hung from the ceiling for color, while pots of live pothos trailed along the room dividers.

"Margarita?" Clint asked.

"Better not. Just in case."

A smile shot across his face. "Right. Here's hoping." He lifted his water glass in a toast.

The waiter hurried over. "Can I get you something to drink? We have pitchers of margaritas on special tonight."

"Iced water for me," Rachel said.

Clint raised his eyebrows at her. "Beer?"

"Please do."

As soon as he ordered his drink, another server set salsa and chips on their table.

"Boy, can't complain about the service." He looked around. "If the food is as good, I'll be coming here often."

Rachel went still. He spoke as though he lived in town, or planned to, or planned to visit often. Could he be different from her dad? Could she dare to hope?

And what would the school board make of that?

She shook away the negativity, determined not to spoil the evening. She wasn't even pregnant yet. Probably. Clint might disappear in a puff of smoke, whichever way the news came out. Ambition might keep him anchored in Los Angeles. She didn't expect him to give up his life, career or ambitions. She hadn't asked that of him and wouldn't.

He thanked the waiter for his beer and talked about the heat of the salsa while she reined in her anxiety about the future. One step at a time.

Clint raised his glass to her. "Here's to our first date—a little late, admittedly. And to our success."

She lifted her water glass off the table, hesitating. "Is it too early? I don't want to jinx anything."

"I have a good feeling, Rachel. Think positive."

"Okay." She clinked her plastic glass to his then took out her phone. If she was pregnant, she wanted a picture to show her child his or her daddy. If she was already pregnant, she might see Clint only casually in the future, despite his grand talk of being a role model. "Say cheese."

His face showed surprise, then he said, "Happy Conception Day" and smiled.

She giggled and had to shoot another picture. She turned on the video feature. Her future kid may not want to think about his or her parents having sex, but Rachel wanted to cherish the memory of this man. "Say that again."

He lifted his glass in another toast. "To our success in the bedroom. And our continued efforts."

She laughed.

"Until we get it right." He winked.

Yeah, her future kid would definitely cringe seeing his bio-dad talk about its conception. Rachel turned off the phone and placed it on the table.

The waiter appeared as though summoned. "It's a birthday? A promotion at work?"

"No, no." Rachel's cheeks flamed. Surely he hadn't overheard? She didn't want any attention directed their way.

"But we are celebrating," Clint told him.

The waiter held out his hand. "Then you need a photo to remember this day."

Rachel's gaze locked on Clint's, which went soft.

"Yeah," he said. "I think we do."

He came to her side of the table and scooted in close, his arm around her shoulders.

"Take a couple, please." She wanted to be able to delete the ones with stars in her eyes. No sense being silly about it. This was almost a business arrangement. Not romance, anyway.

"Thank you," Clint said as the waiter handed back the phone and rushed to another table. He leaned close and kissed her softly. "Here's to our success. I do feel good about it, Rachel. I'm not saying I felt anything mystical, but..." He shrugged.

"I know." She squeezed his hand. "I hope so too."

Except then she might never see him again.

He moved back to his side of the table and the dinner conversation changed to their respective jobs. They had a regular date, with great food and great conversation. But in the back of her mind, she wondered if they were joined by a third presence at the table.

The pork carnitas plate with rice and refried beans kept her reaching for her water glass and hoping the possible-embryo liked spicy foods. She turned down a bite of Clint's street tacos, sure she'd spill the contents down her clothes. Besides, she had plenty to eat.

She scraped the last of the beans up with a chip from the basket and sighed.

"I can't believe I ate all that." She cringed. Why did she point out her unladylike appetite?

"It was too good to leave behind." Clint stretched and patted his belly. Not a speck of food on his shirt. "Ready?"

She couldn't contain her smile. "Should we go home and" —she waggled her eyebrows— "continue the celebration?"

"Yes, ma'am." He grinned as he rose beside her. "If one, two or three weren't, then the fourth time will definitely be the charm."

"I'm a little nervous."

Rachel's heart clenched. Good lord, he was cute.

"We've done this before," she reminded him, hands gentle on his shoulders as he stretched out over her. "Last night, twice. This morning. A few weeks ago."

"Oh, trust me. I remember." He kissed her nose. "But this time it counts. This time, it's about making new life. Taking an irrevocable step into the future."

"Oh great. Now I'm nervous."

"You? You only have to lay back and enjoy it."

"I plan to." She looped her arms behind his neck with a grin. "If past performances are any indication, I definitely will."

Clint's quick kiss proved his distraction. "I have to make sure I'm sending you healthy sperm. The strong swimmers with a lot of good-looking DNA. And senses of humor. And artistic ability."

"Wow, that's a tall order." She settled beneath him and let him talk it out. Was he joking to ease her tension or did nerves really have him by the throat?

She could take him by the throat—with her teeth. His strong tanned body pressing against her didn't encourage chatter. Her muscles softened to cushion him. Her body readied to accept him. Her heart pounded out a promise to protect him.

Oh, hold on.

She wasn't going all gooey over Clint Walker. The man basically had "moving on" in his name. *Her* heart had to be protected, and she wasn't stupid enough to think sex equaled love and happily ever after.

But God, he was adorable. She smoothed a strand of his platinum hair from his forehead, feeling tender. "I hope our baby has your green eyes."

He started. "What?"

"Your eyes. They're mesmerizing. Sexy."

Tension eased from his body and he rested more comfortably against her length. "Thanks for the compliment, but I don't want my daughter to have sexy eyes."

"What about your son?"

"That's fine. He might need some advantage in case he's stupid."

"Hey! My son is not going to be stupid."

"Hopefully, he'll get your smart genes."

"Your looks, my brains."

"Your looks, your brains," he corrected.

Rachel shook her head. "Your dazzling hair, not my plain brown."

He picked up a strand and kissed it. "Shiny brown. So many colors swirling through. It's anything but plain." He kissed her nose, a habit she thought she'd hate but found kind of endearing. "Besides," he continued, "our daughter is going from her all-girls school into a convent."

Rachel made a scoffing sound. "Sorry, cowboy, not gonna happen."

He scowled, definitely joking now. "So she'll be a spinster taking care of her parents all her life? At least my way, she gets the fulfillment of being of service."

"Right. As long as she doesn't have sex."

He winced. "Don't even talk about that. She isn't even born yet."

Rachel cocked an eyebrow. "And does our son have to go into the monastery?"

"Well, no." He cleared his throat. "But I'll teach him about being safe."

"You're such a hypocrite."

"Well, you've got at least sixteen years to make me see the light."

Her gut clenched. When he talked about the future, she could almost believe him. She wanted to. Theirs wasn't a conventional arrangement. Heck, they hadn't known each other a month. But the bond between them held her fast. She wanted to think he'd still be around on some prom night in the future. Either he'd live with her as her partner or come over to her house to worry about the kid being out too late.

Stop it, Rachel. That's a pipe dream.

She knew better. Men didn't stay. Not her dad. Not her

mom's second husband. Certainly not Henry, her ex. And not Clint. They were joking around about the future, not making promises.

He nuzzled her cheek, trailing kisses and warmth to her ear. Tingles brushed over her skin.

Stay in the moment. This is what you have—all you have—for certain.

For now, it would be enough.

The next morning, Clint dragged his feet about leaving. The sun had risen too early and the plane waiting for him to board would arrive at the airport too soon. He wanted to stay with her, to ensure Rachel conceived. Not only for the physical act, which he enjoyed the hell out of, but he needed to uphold his end of the bargain. He wouldn't rest easy until he knew she was pregnant.

And if that realization didn't make his head spin, he didn't know what would.

He glanced over to where she sat on the side of the bed, jotting a note on a pad on her nightstand. A filmy emerald robe gaped in front to expose her over-sized gray University of Colorado sleep shirt. The hem rode up on her thighs, enticing him. *Stay*, her body seemed to demand. Even her pink toenail polish called his name. *You're needed here. Why are you leaving?*

Good question.

Clint abandoned his packing and crossed the bedroom. She glanced at him, eyebrows raised in question. He pulled her up and into his arms.

"Maybe I can take a few more days of vacation," he suggested as he nuzzled her neck. She was warm and soft and smelled like some old-fashioned flower. "I could stay here a little longer, while you're fertile."

She pulled back and glanced at him, an amused look on her face. "What do you know about fertility? Been reading up?"

He buried his face in her neck again so she wouldn't witness his flush of guilt. She wouldn't accuse him of being an idiot. She'd think it was cute, which was much worse in his opinion. "I just don't want to leave you hanging."

"You did your part." She actually rubbed his shoulder consolingly, like a six-year-old who'd scraped a knee. "Now I have to hope one of the sperm does its job."

"*I*" have to hope? She'd already blocked him from the process. He didn't feel used, exactly. Good God, he wasn't a girl. But...

What? But *what*, he demanded of himself.

Coming up blank— He winced. The word "blank" wasn't even allowed to enter his mind. Not coming up with an answer, he corrected himself, he shook off his sense of something being wrong. "Okay. I guess I do need to get back to work tomorrow."

"Of course you do." Rachel put a light hand on his arm. "This was the plan all along. I don't want you to think I'm upset."

But why aren't you? He gave her a smile and a slight nod that must have appeared convincing because she turned back to her side table and list making. His mind gave a grunt of dissatisfaction as he crammed a shirt into his duffel bag. If Rachel wasn't concerned about his leaving, he darn well shouldn't be.

Nevertheless, her easy acceptance of his departure grated against his skin.

They had a quick breakfast—stiff and awkward on his part, light and breezy on hers. Now he almost couldn't wait to leave. To escape her nonchalance. To stop feeling like the emotional one. This was so unlike him. He wasn't a "love 'em and leave 'em" type, but he didn't linger where he wasn't wanted.

"I don't know how to say this, Clint, but thank you." Rachel shrugged. "That sounds so inadequate."

He knocked on the wooden counter, a little superstitious niggle urging him to do so. "Don't thank me yet. We don't know if it took."

"That's not the point. I don't have the right words to tell

you what it means to me that you would volunteer to help. This is a big deal and I want you to know that. You're a special guy."

Uncomfortable, he winked at her. "Having sex with you is no hardship, believe me."

"It's a huge gesture, so don't brush it off. And no matter the outcome of this weekend, I want you to know how touched I am that you'd try. I want a baby so badly, and having it with your sperm instead of a stranger's is such a relief."

That faint compliment made him smile. "And the delivery system is better, too, right?"

She chuckled and buttered her toast. Disappointment slashed through him.

Maybe he was a girl, after all.

CHAPTER SIX

August

Rachel set her cloth tote bag on the kitchen table and blew out a breath, as though she were an international spy who'd escaped capture. She hadn't been caught, but then, she'd shopped for her purchases two towns away. In three different stores.

Feeling silly, she slid the boxes onto the table surface, grinning as the five pregnancy tests emerged. Five. Maybe she'd overdone it. One test was absolutely not a sure enough answer, however, so she didn't feel bad about buying test number two. Then, one also had to consider that test one detected a pregnancy the earliest—so could that answer be trusted? And if she couldn't trust test one, as it was too soon to know for sure and if one result wasn't enough, then she'd *had* to buy three, right? Stood to reason. Only logical.

But the other two?

She covered her face with her hands and scrubbed away

the crazy, laughing a little. She'd admit it, to the empty room, anyway, that she was a little bit obsessed.

If she'd been braver, she wouldn't have had to wait this long, but testing after only a few days would have tempted fate. The earliest test available could have predicted her pregnancy status before Clint even got his clothes on, more or less. But she hadn't trusted the speed of its results.

However, she needed to know. Not only for herself, but if the worse came to pass—she knocked on the wooden cabinet for luck—she'd need to inform Clint and check if they could meet up for another round of baby-making during her next fertile period.

God, she wished he were here now to share this moment. He'd want to celebrate the good news with her, of course. But if no line appeared or the "not pregnant" or the blue or pink or whatever indicated failure, she'd have to put on a brave face for him, and she wasn't sure if she could.

Hopefully, she'd be calling him with good news instead.

Eyes closed for a moment, she took another deep breath to steady her nerves then slid down into a chair to study the boxes. She'd done her research online and with the doctors at the fertility clinic, and had already read the boxes in the store. But she lined up each in order of when she could take the test for greatest accuracy. The earliest test she would take tomorrow, since morning urine contained the most concentrated HCG, the indicator she carried a fetus. Or didn't.

Waiting for her missed period would be a more normal and reliable indicator, but would throw off her schedule. Still, she had to accept that if this first try with Clint hadn't worked, next month might not either. She might never get pregnant the conventional way.

Rachel twirled the box in her fingers. It did say she could test any time of day. Morning was best, but... And she had four more tests if this result was inconclusive. She wouldn't believe a positive result on just one test, hence the five boxes in front of her. Maybe her purchases hadn't been so crazy after all.

"Heck with it," she muttered, grabbing up two boxes.

Once in the bathroom, she re-read the already-memorized instructions, washed her hands and winked at herself in the mirror. "You can do this."

Do what? Pee on a stick? Become pregnant? Face a negative response?

Blood drained from her face. No. She wouldn't psyche herself out of taking the test. She and her reflection nodded decisively. Rachel smiled at herself. This might be the last time she viewed the image in the mirror and saw a childless woman. Everything might change.

"Just do it already," her reflection chided. Shaking her head, Rachel set up everything then did as directed, but found it hard to release her flow. She laughed at herself—too scared to pee! Laughing did the trick.

She gulped as destiny was launched. Checking the time, she started the countdown. She finished and straightened her clothes, not wanting to become a mother with her pants around her ankles.

The seconds ticked backward, or so it seemed. Then it was time to look. Time to know, one way or the other. She blew out a breath and checked the result.

And burst into tears.

Rachel keyed in Clint's cell phone number and held her breath. Anticipation crept under her skin like barbed spiders. Maybe she should have done a video call so she could see his face. He'd be happy. He'd be done with his part of this venture. He'd be out of her life.

She frowned. That wasn't a positive.

Just as she thought to hang up rather than leave a voice mail, he answered.

"Hey, Rachel. I was thinking about calling you. But I didn't want to…you know. How are you?"

She answered something generic, wondering what he didn't want to do or say. Because despite his assertion, she didn't "you know" what he meant.

"So, any news yet?" He gulped audibly through the phone, his tight voice making him sound as nervous to hear the news as she was to tell him. "Did we do it right?"

Relieved to hear the Clint she knew, Rachel grinned. "Bingo."

"Bingo?"

"I'm pregnant."

"Oh my God. Rachel, that's amazing. That's great." He went silent for a moment, and she wished she could see his expression. She should have made this a video call. He took a deep breath in. Cleared his throat. "I'm so happy for you. For us."

She swiped tears from her cheeks. "Me too."

"When is little Bingo due?"

She laughed. "We are not naming our baby Bingo!"

Our baby. Our baby.

The words echoed through the room, through her heart, and across the distance dividing them.

Clint cleared his throat again. Silence hummed between them with words unsaid. Words she wished she could say. Wished he would. Wished were true between them.

Now she was glad she hadn't done a video call. Her face would probably give her away. It was hormones, of course. They didn't have that kind of relationship, and she wouldn't pressure him into anything just because she was pregnant with his baby.

Tears welled in her eyes. *Pregnant.* She put a hand on her

flat stomach. A fetus swam around down there, undetectable by touch.

Clint's part was over. Her job was now to take care of this precious little collection of cells as it grew into a human.

"You did a great job," she told him, grateful. She didn't have words to express her appreciation.

"You too," Clint said. "I'm sorry I'm not there to celebrate with you. To… I don't know. Hold you."

"I know. I'd like that too."

"Hey," his voice brightened. "We can still celebrate. Didn't we buy some sparkling cider when I was there? We can toast our success. Toast little Bingo."

She laughed. "We aren't calling him Bingo."

"What if it's a girl?"

"Then definitely not."

Clint made a thoughtful *hmm* sound. "We'll have to talk about that, I guess."

"I don't know about having cider. Sounds kind of sour."

"Are you having morning sickness?"

"No, not yet. But why take chances? I have sparkling water."

"Good enough. Let's get our drinks and toast our success."

They updated each other as they separately found glasses and poured their drinks. "My last beer," Clint said.

"You'll have to get more." Rachel slipped an ice cube into her glass.

"No, I mean, I'll stop drinking too. It's only fair."

"That's plain weird." She put the bottle back in the fridge. "You don't have any restrictions."

He didn't say anything while she swirled her glass, making the drink cold. His prolonged silence caught her attention. "Clint?"

"Right," he said. It came out flat.

"I mean," she scrambled for words, "I appreciate the solidarity, but I don't want you to feel…"

What? Beholden? Responsible? Involved? Trapped?

"Like you have to suffer," she finished.

"Not a big deal either way."

"I appreciate the thought—"

"Just drop it, Rachel."

"Sorry."

A moment passed. She was already saying the wrong things, upsetting him, driving him away.

"I have my glass if you're ready," she ventured.

"I'll click mine against the phone. You do the same."

"Okay."

"To Bingo." A smile rang through Clint's voice.

Relieved to hear it and be back on firm ground with him, she let his teasing soak in. "To Bingo." She tapped her glass against her cell phone to make a little noise and heard him do the same. "And to the best donor ever. Thank you, Clint."

"To you, Rachel." The tap came through the receiver. "Thanks for including me in this. It's a miracle."

Tears stuck in her throat. "It is. It really is."

Clint lowered his phone to the side table as though laying down an egg. Apt, he thought when he recognized the extreme care he took. An egg; a baby. Both would need care and nurturing and watchful eyes to ensure its safety.

And he wouldn't be a part of any of that.

He dropped into a chair and rubbed his hands over his face. God knew, he was beyond thrilled for Rachel. Her dream had been achieved. In a few months, she'd be a mother and cradle her child in her arms.

Except that child was *their* child. His child.

And only Rachel would cuddle it.

Only Rachel would nurture it.

Only Rachel would see it grow into a delightful little person. Experience its first word, first steps, first…everything.

Clint ground his back teeth. God, he was a bastard. He should be happy right now. Victorious. They'd done it. On the first try… Well, maybe the fourth try but on the first weekend of trying. Not all hopeful parents-to-be were that lucky. So, "yay."

He just hadn't expected to feel this possessive of the baby. To feel this envious of Rachel. To feel this cheated.

He slammed a fist into the arm of the chair. *Get over it.* He'd gone into this deal with his eyes open. Envy and jealousy had no part in her happy news. Rachel's dream had come true, and he'd participated in the baby-making most happily.

He snorted. Oh, yeah. He'd been eager enough then. Felt like a fricking hero for helping her. Even recognizing that she'd wanted to parent solo, he'd agreed.

He just hadn't anticipated this feeling of…loss.

Now what was he going to do?

Talking to Jack was out of the question because no one had been told yet. His friends in L.A. wouldn't understand. The guys would consider this a near miss: almost getting "caught" in BabyLandia. His women friends would eye him like a pariah, leaving "poor" Rachel stuck with a baby, no matter that she'd asked for exactly that. They wouldn't understand his devastation when he'd felt her creating a distance across the phone line, pushing him away.

He wouldn't be a father, and he wanted to shout the news to everyone. To anyone. He wanted to pass out cigars or whatever the modern day equivalent was.

But he wasn't going to be a dad. He was a sperm donor, providing the means to an end. He had basically stood at stud—useful to a point and then not needed.

Only a jerk would be whining, he thought with disgust. It wasn't as though he'd been used, and it certainly hadn't been against his will.

He brought up a search engine on his phone, found what he wanted, and hit Call.

A perky voice answered. "It's a rosy day at Beach Petals. How may I help you?"

"I need to order some flowers."

Breathless from racing into the living room, Rachel grabbed up the phone on its sixth ring. She didn't carry her cell phone with her from room to room, but she might have to start doing so. In a few months, she wouldn't be able to run anywhere. The heat of the August day didn't help. "Hello?"

"Hey," her cousin Grace bubbled into the receiver.

"Hey, yourself." Rachel settled onto the couch for a chat, a little disappointed the caller wasn't Clint. She glanced at the flowers he'd sent in celebration. The card read only "Bingo!" and made her smile. "Where are you? Still in Little Tree?"

"Yep. Mike's started the horse farm and his brother and sister are still living with us."

"Us?"

Grace giggled. "Yeah. We're being terrible role models. It took Mike two seconds to decide they were old enough to deal with it."

"That's a surprise." Her friend Mike had been an overprotective older brother for as long as Rachel had known him.

"Fortunately, he can no longer resist me."

Rachel had to laugh. "Who can?"

"He made a good effort for way too long, if you ask me. But now we're deliriously happy."

"I'd like to see what that looks like on Mike." Rachel was pretty darn happy for them and for herself, but she wasn't ready to share her news.

"Can you travel?" Grace asked, as though she could read Rachel's mind. "I mean, I don't know how that whole getting pregnant thing works. How's it going with the donor? Any results yet? Or is it not the right time to try?"

Rachel bit her lip, yearning to blurt out the truth. She wanted to shout her news from the rooftops, but especially wanted to share with her family. Grace would support her, had up to this point, and Rachel felt a little guilty about hiding the truth. But little Bingo was too fragile to tempt Fate.

Wait. She had *not* just thought of her child as "Bingo." She laid a hand on her stomach and mouthed, "Sorry."

She said to Grace, "I'll tell you when I can. The donor is still being wonderful. Patient and kind. And tender and funny."

Silence pulsed for a minute.

"You're falling for him," Grace said quietly.

"No. It's not like that."

"Is that wise?" she continued as though Rachel hadn't denied her feelings.

"I'm not. I mean, I feel fond of him, of course. Grateful. He's doing me a huge favor. And there's a certain intimacy involved. It's not like using a turkey baster, you know."

Grace's laugh came through the line. "Are you going to share details?"

"Ick. No."

"Yeah, *ick* on that baster part. Please don't. I was hoping more for details of what he looks like. What your future kid will look like."

"He's tall, blond and handsome. Great body. Strong. Good genes for" —Bingo— "the baby to inherit."

"Sounds delicious. Does he have a name?"

"Not one that I'm telling you."

"I'll call him TB then."

Rachel wrinkled her nose in disgust. "Like tuberculosis?"

"Oh. No, TB like turkey baster, but now that you've put tuberculosis in my mind, I can't call him that."

"That would be ominous." Rachel knocked on the wooden end table next to the couch to scare away any omens of illness.

"Oh my gosh, I almost forgot to tell you why I called," Grace blurted. "I'm getting married."

Rachel's hold on the phone tightened with her surprise. "What? You are? To Mike? That's fabulous. When?"

"Of course to Mike. As for when... In about ten minutes now."

"What!"

Grace's laugh came through the phone. "I know, it's insane. We're insane."

"I didn't even know he'd proposed. Why didn't you tell me things were that serious?"

"Oh, the proposal! That's a great story, and I can't wait to tell you, except my husband-to-be is right here, and I've got about two seconds before I have to go into the courthouse."

"Courthouse?"

"We're eloping." Grace giggled. "Is it called that when you rush off to the justice of the peace? Maybe we're just getting married in a hurry."

Dread shook Grace. "Why are you in a hurry?"

"Not for that reason—not for your reason. We just love each other, and we're living together already in front of the kids, and there's no reason to wait. Oh, I do wish you could have been here though. But Mike asked yesterday what kind of wedding I had in mind, and I think I scared twenty years off his life when I said 'the quick kind.'"

Rachel could picture the scene. Mike Thompson was nothing if not steady and dependable. "Are you sure you're not rushing things? You didn't even know him two months ago."

Silence stretched between them. Two months ago, Grace had been ready to marry another man, Clint's brother, Jack. She'd been in the dress, at the church.

"How long do you have to know someone to know it's the real thing?" Grace said.

An image of Clint popped into her mind. Not long, she wanted to say. But that was hormones and gratitude. Rachel shook her head. "I wouldn't know. Never had the real thing."

"There's no schedule for falling in love that I know about, and even if there were—"

"You would ignore it."

Grace laughed. "Exactly. And I'm sure about this, Rach. Mike's the guy for me, the one I want to make happy and drive crazy for the rest of our lives."

"Well, I couldn't be more thrilled for you. Congratulations, to you both. Tell Mike for me, okay?

"Hey, Mike," Grace called. "Rachel says you're a lucky S.O.B. to get me."

"Grace!" Rachel couldn't help laughing.

"What was that, Rachel?" Grace said, though not into the phone. "He better treat me right or you'll come here and do what to him?"

Rachel shook her head. "'Drive him crazy' is right."

"Don't worry, he has his moments of revenge. But at least

he swears at me in Spanish, so I can ignore him." Grace laughed. "Okay, okay. He says to tell you I'm only kidding about him swearing at me."

"And the wedding is in a few minutes?"

"Just waiting for Lexi and Jack."

"What?"

"Well, who but my sister would be my matron of honor? I would have had you as my bridesmaid, along with Mike's sister, Anita, but we didn't have time to plan anything."

"Is this the wedding you want?" Rachel recalled the planning Grace had put into her wedding to Jack.

"I had a big wedding already," Grace said, her shrug almost audible. "Now I'm going to marry the man of my dreams. Of my heart."

"I'm happy for you, Grace. I really am. For both of you. I'm sorry I couldn't be there, but I understand. When it's right, it's right." She thought of her own plan to have a baby, and how certain she'd felt about having Clint as her donor. She thought of Lexi stepping in to marry Jack when Grace jilted him. Maybe all the Marshall women went full-tilt after their dreams. "You have to do what your heart demands."

"Thank you. It's so perfect that you said that. I love you."

"Love you too. Oh, and Grace?"

"Yes?"

"Make sure you stick around for this one."

CHAPTER SEVEN

Rachel swung open the door Thursday and launched herself at Clint. He staggered backward from the surprise while his arms tightened around her.

"Sorry," she said, still hugging his neck.

"Not a problem." His arms tightened. "I'll do better anticipating this the next time."

She eased back to her toes, maintaining her smile. It was easy to say "next time." Good intentions and all that because he was an honorable man. But something would come up. Their visits would dwindle to phone calls to texts to…nothing. She couldn't expect him to stay around now that his part was done. Her own father hadn't stuck around, and Clint hadn't agreed to any strings. His staying by her side forever had never been part of the game plan.

"I'm glad you could stop over on your way to Montana." Rachel held the door for him to bring his duffel inside.

"I had to work like the devil this week to get tomorrow

off," Clint said, "but it'll be worth it to celebrate with Annabeth in person. I've missed so many of her birthdays."

"You fly out tomorrow?" She couldn't keep the disappointment from her voice. Gesturing to the couch, she took a seat.

"Yeah. Sorry about that."

"No, I'm glad you came. How old is Annabeth?"

He sat facing her. "Seven. We FaceTime, but I'm curious to see in person how she's changed. Now that she has a stepmom, she might be a little more girly than shows on a screen."

Rachel smiled, thinking of her cousin. "I doubt it. Lexi was a tomboy and still isn't much into traditional girly stuff."

"Well, besides the housekeeper, Annabeth's only had Jack and Uncle Crusty for guidance, so anything will be an improvement."

"What did you get her?"

After a wince, Clint ran a hand down his face and peeked at her over his fingers. The crinkles around his eyes proved he hid a smile. "A basketball."

She couldn't help but laugh.

"And shoes, and workout clothes. Not girly," he admitted with a shrug, "but L.A. chic."

"That probably counts."

He leaned in. "Can I touch your stomach? I know it's

weird, but—"

She took his hand and laid his palm on her. "You can't feel anything yet. And it's not weird. I'm doing this all the time."

His expression went soft and he stared with wonder, though there was no difference yet. "I can't believe it. I'm so happy for you, Rachel."

Her insides turned mushy with tenderness. "Have I said thank you? Because I can't say it enough. And thank you for the flowers. They were perfect."

"You're welcome. And you're welcome." He smiled. "But the first part was truly my pleasure. Have you told anyone yet?"

She shook her head. "It's early. I want to make sure it sticks."

He nodded. "That's why I sent the flowers. To say thank you for letting me be part of it, and congratulations. I didn't want you to feel alone."

Her heart melted. Clint was such a great guy. Memories of the baby-making rushed through her and lust flared. "Want to go upstairs and touch my flat stomach…without the blouse in the way?"

He drew back. "Uh…"

She raised her eyebrows, delighted at his surprise. "No? You want to do it here, on the couch? My goodness, you are bold."

He jumped—no other word for it—to his feet. "Uh, no. I mean, of course I do. But no. I thought we'd go to dinner. To celebrate."

She stood, a little disappointed but touched. "I guess I can wait until after dinner."

"Yeah. About that." He stopped.

Rachel stepped backward, uneasy. Something in his tone shot off warning signals. "What about that?"

"I booked a late afternoon flight tomorrow so we can go shopping first. And Jack always has me doing chores first thing I get to the ranch. Every morning. I need some sleep tonight to catch up."

"Sleep."

"Yeah. I mean, I'd love to, you know, be with you. But I've been working all hours at my job to get time off, to get home for Annabeth's birthday, and I'm beat."

"No, I understand. Of course."

And she was afraid she did understand. This was the first sign of Clint easing away. Soon he'd be no more than a shadow, a memory. Like her father.

"Are you feeling up for dinner?" Clint asked. "Food not disagreeing with you, I hope."

He looked miserable and sorry and nervous.

The bastard.

If he'd been callous, she would be glad to see him go. But not Clint. He had to be…such a good friend. Ugh.

She drew in a breath. This man had given her the greatest gift possible. She couldn't be angry with him. He was living up to their agreement, the terms she'd set: only sex, no strings, no romantic relationship.

Rachel put on a smile. "I'm starving."

Rachel trooped through the baby furniture aisles the next morning, trying to rein in Clint. He wanted everything he saw. More endearingly, he'd done his research. He'd asked friends what the baby would need and use versus what items were superfluous. He'd checked reviews and product warnings. He probably knew more about baby paraphernalia than she did.

If only she could figure him out. Furniture shopping didn't seem like something a man did if he wanted to distance himself from the situation.

He approached the row of baby beds like a general on a battlefield.

"Can't have Bingo falling out." He shook the crib. Hard. It rattled and bounced side to side.

"Clint," she hissed, looking around for someone approaching to throw them out of the store. "Stop that."

He shook another. "I want a good sturdy one. The best."

She did too, but the best would be out of her price range.

She glanced at the price of the first bed he shook then tried not to stagger backward at the amount. "Not this one."

"Why not?"

"Bad vibes."

He smoothed the quick frown of confusion from between his brows. "Okay."

She ambled pseudo-casually down the row, trying not to be obvious about reading the price tags. That wasn't an argument she wanted to have in the store. Several cribs down, the prices read more in the range of her wallet. "What about this one?"

Clint shook his head. "Not dark brown. Or black."

Amused, she asked, "You're thinking pastels?"

"Or white. Something light and cheerful." He shrugged. "Baby colors."

"Why, Clint Walker, for all your California ways, you're a traditionalist."

After a moment where he looked ready to refute it, he nodded. "Probably. I am from Montana."

"What's that got to do with it?"

"Traditional values. Our family ranch house is over one hundred and fifty years old or more. I'd have to ask Crusty." He shook another crib. "He probably laid the cornerstone when it was built."

She laughed and decided to enjoy the day. If this were to

be their last together, she would have fun and build memories. Planning their baby's room together made her chest ache.

This could well be the end of their in-person relationship. After dinner last night, he'd pleaded a hard work week and slept in the guest room. The sign of a man with one foot out the door.

So. Now that she'd conceived the baby, there wouldn't be any more sex. His job was complete. Which she understood. They didn't have a relationship, weren't in love, had never dated other than the one time during their baby-making weekend. But she'd never heard of a man who turned down no-strings sex. It wasn't like she'd get *more* pregnant. Rachel had to surmise he'd lost interest in her.

She had to fight him on who would pay for the crib—*she would*—and on what she could afford. Their first argument, and about money, the hardest of subjects.

He ground his teeth when she continued to return items to the shelves.

"I want to buy something for the baby," he said.

"Fine." She turned on him with heat burning her face. "He'll need baby bottles. They're in some other aisle. Go there. Now."

Clint reeled back a step.

She turned away from him, frustrated with them both. "Sorry."

"I didn't know you had a temper."

She took a breath and turned to him. "I also have a limited budget. You helping with the conception saved me a bunch, but I don't want to waste it on things the baby won't need. Having the best of the line of beds is a nice idea, but I just want a good quality, safe, and sturdy crib." She took another breath. "I feel like you're pushing me."

"And I feel like you're pushing me away."

Shocked, she could only stare.

"I only want to buy something for my baby—for your baby that I helped make," he corrected.

"I never meant to leave you out of decisions," she whispered, stricken with guilt. "I just can't overspend."

"Let's see what we can find together. Not too expensive, but not too cheap."

"Deal."

"I'll find the bottles."

Rachel stared after him. Was this his goodbye present? Buying something to ease his guilt? Why should he feel guilty? The man confused her on so many levels.

On Sunday, Clint watched Annabeth open the second to last present on the pile, which was from him. He'd packed the clothes and shoes around the basketball to disguise its shape, and it seemed to have worked.

Annabeth, now seven, laughed as she discovered the ball inside.

"Wow, Uncle Clint." She beamed at him, a space now replacing a lost tooth, as she ran a hand over the workout clothes. "These shorts are perfect. The shoes are awesome. And they're in my team colors."

She held the top up to her and spread the pants over her lap.

"I can return it and send you the right size if I guessed wrong." Clint had called the housekeeper ahead of time for guidance, but he wanted to give Annabeth a graceful way to refuse if she didn't like his present.

"This looks right." She gathered it in her fists and made to rise. "I'll go try it on now."

"Not right now, sugar cube," Jack said. "You have other gifts to open."

Annabeth glanced at Lexi, who shook her head. Interesting. Had she thought her step-mom of three months would override Jack?

"A basketball?" Crusty made a harrumphing noise. "Don't you know nothing about girls? She wants perfume."

"I really don't, Uncle Crusty," Annabeth said.

"She's too young for perfume," Jack countered.

Crusty scowled harder. "Then give her something all kids want. An Eyebox or whatever it's called."

Clint couldn't help laughing. "An eyebox?"

Crusty formed a rectangular shape on his lap with his arthritic hands. "You know, like a plate, only a rectangle, and they play music on it."

"Wow," Clint teased. "So not-even-close."

"It's pretty close," Annabeth, always the peacekeeper, put in. Lexi bit her lip and Jack looked away, mouth twitching into a grin. The girl turned to smile at Crusty. "But really, Uncle Crusty, I'm happy with the basketball and sports clothes Uncle Clint brought all the way from Los Angeles. I'll be the only player at practice wearing something this cool."

"Maybe," Crusty grumbled.

"You know so much about kids? What did you get her, old man?" Clint gestured to the flat box smaller than a pack of gum. The geezer had a soft heart and loved Annabeth more than he'd ever shown love for anyone else. That didn't discount his cantankerous side, which a generous person might call eccentric.

"Go ahead." Crusty nodded to Annabeth.

She peeled off the wrapping as though the paper itself was the present. She smiled then looked at Crusty with a "what did you do?" look on her face.

In her hand she held a matchbox. Not a toy car but an actual box that had once, or maybe even still, held matches.

Good lord. If Crusty thought an iPad was an "eyebox" for

music, what did he think she'd use a matchbox for?

Crusty jerked his chin, indicating she should continue. Annabeth slid open the inside shelf and stared.

"What is it, Anna?" Lexi asked.

Clint blinked, reminded again that Lexi had shortened his niece's name to fit the pint-sized girl. And *Anna* loved it. Maybe because it was hard to be reminded of her biological mother, Sarabeth, who had died when Annabeth was three and whom she didn't remember.

Anna held up a piece of soft brown leather the size of a quarter. "I'm not sure."

All eyes turned toward Crusty.

"Well, I couldn't wrap it."

"Couldn't wrap what, Uncle Crusty?" Anna asked.

"Your new saddle, o' course."

Her mouth dropped open.

"It were your mother's." He glanced at Lexi. "Your first mother's, I mean."

Anna burst into tears. The adults in the room froze as she covered her face with both hands and wailed. Lexi grabbed Jack's arm as he made to go to her and pulled him back onto the sofa.

Clint's chest went tight, his breathing constricting as grief returned. Sarabeth had gone out riding alone one day. The horse returned to the ranch late, with no sign of a rider, who should have been seated in the very saddle Crusty thought would make such a great gift.

Teeth clenched, Jack said, "I threw that out."

His jaw jutted forward, Crusty said, "And I saved it. Kep' it in the loft so's you couldn't do that again."

"It's old," Jack countered, his expression bleak. "Probably cracked and dried hard."

"You sayin' I don't know how to take care of tack?"

With only her dark blue eyes peeking out between her fingers, Anna stumbled her way across the living room to Crusty and curled onto his lap, her head on his shoulder. He patted her as though this were an everyday occurrence.

"Thank you, Uncle Crusty. Thank you," she choked out. "That's so per-per-perfect. Just what I—"

Sobs overtook her.

Lexi, tears in her own eyes, nodded at Jack with a wobbly smile. He took a breath and made a visible show of relaxing.

"He took it pretty good," Crusty said to Lexi.

Jack turned to her. "You *knew*?"

"She brung down the saddle so's I could oil it up. Didn't want me to maneuver on that ladder, though I coulda."

Lexi threw her hands up. "Thanks a lot, Crusty. You just threw me under the bus."

"Don't see why I should take all the blame."

Anna sat up. "Can I go see it?"

"Sure," Lexi said, eagerness to escape the drama—and fallout—showing in the way she jumped to her feet.

"You too." Anna handed Crusty his cane.

"Be faster without me," he grumbled. But he inched forward on the sofa to get his feet under him.

"We can go slow." Anna smiled at him, then turned to Jack. "Daddy?"

Her question relayed as much about his mental state as his permission or acceptance.

"I'll catch up."

"I'll be sure he does," Clint said. When the trio was out of sight, he went to the wet bar, poured two whiskeys, and handed one to his brother. They'd been through the dark days of Sarabeth's death and dealing with a toddler. Caring after Annabeth had probably kept Jack sane or at least sober.

Jack took the glass with an explosion of breath. As he threw back his shot, Clint said his goodbye to that intense grief, believing it would be softer as it came to visit in the future. Lexi had helped them all there. He poured one more shot for each of them, raising his glass this time. "To Sarabeth."

"To Sarabeth." Jack drank it straight and fast. "I'll always love her."

"We all know that." Clint included Lexi in that collective "we" and Jack nodded.

"I never thought I'd be this happy again."

Clint chuckled. "Maybe we should drink a toast to Grace, in thanks for jilting you."

Jack snorted. "I do owe her, I guess. But we've had enough."

Clint watched Jack's expression as his brother looked toward the door. "Are you ready for this, Jack? Is it really okay with you?"

Jack filled his cheeks then let go of the breath. "Can't say I wouldn't have appreciated a heads up, but... Yeah. I'll come around to thinking it was a good idea."

"Kind of sweet that Lexi was in on it." Clint tried to ease the way for his sister-in-law. "Accepting Annabeth's love for both her mothers."

"That woman." But humor and love layered through Jack's voice. "She'd have done it anyway, even if I had objected, because it was right for Anna."

"You go ahead," Clint said, giving the family a moment. "I want to use the facilities."

"Don't be long."

Clint filled his glass with water and leaned back against the fireplace. So much for not drinking while Rachel was pregnant. But he'd needed this, needed to share the moment and memory with Jack, and put it behind them. Still a part of their past, but not as painful now.

The weekend had been hard for him, and he kicked

himself for it. Celebrating the pregnancy and then shopping with Rachel on Friday had been torture, knowing she might send him away any minute. She'd agreed he could be a role model and help raise the kid, but neither of them knew how to make that a reality. She probably would have agreed to anything to have him donate to her cause.

Then he'd come here to a happy home, and being a part but not a part of it had torn him up. He wouldn't have this sense of belonging, this *family tie* with his child. He was just DNA.

Seeing Annabeth had underscored that for him. She'd grown. She now answered to a new nickname. She had friends he didn't know and skills he hadn't been around to see her acquire.

He looked at her growing up without him and envisioned his future child growing up without him too. And he didn't like it.

September

Clint waited on Rachel's porch, tempted to knock again. He didn't want to disturb her if she was napping. Planning a surprise stopover at her house had seemed like a fun idea, up until four minutes ago when she didn't answer his first knock. Or his second.

The door opened and Rachel appeared, a powder blue

terry bathrobe clutched under her pale-as-death face. The blood drained from his head as dread leeched every molecule of warmth from his body. Had she lost the baby? What else could make her look this wretched? He gulped. "What's wrong?"

"What are you doing here?" she croaked. Then she stepped back and waved him in. "Get in here. Bingo doesn't like the chilly weather at the moment."

Chilly? It was seventy-five degrees.

"What?" He shut the door behind him, studying her. His knees liquefied and his vision blurred with relief at mention of the baby. Her use of their nickname for the baby didn't pass his attention but now was not the time to tease her. "What's wrong?"

She gave him a sour look. "I'm pregnant."

He regained his sense of humor on an upsurge of happy adrenaline. "I know." He winked. "I was there."

"You're hilarious." Rachel tipped her head back against the wall. "I have morning sickness."

"But it's like two-thirty."

She stared at him as though he deserved a dunce cap.

"Right," he backpedaled. "I guess I've heard you can get it any time of day, right? Sorry. I wasn't thinking. Just surprised."

"I'm sorry." Rachel sighed. "I'm not the nicest person

today. Good thing we have a long weekend so I don't scare the kids. Labor Day. Hah."

He took her arm and led her to the couch, easing her down as though she were made of delicate porcelain. Her face had the same thin, almost see-through quality as fine china. "Have you been sick all day?"

"Couple of days."

"Is it supposed to last that long?" He'd read a book on this, but every word fled his memory when faced with Rachel looking like she'd been wrung out, twisted violently and drained of energy. Rode hard and put away wet, as Crusty would say. And any horseman knew that didn't bode well.

"It's fine, Clint. Normal." She squinted at him as she reached toward the end table for a plain cracker and glass of what smelled like apple juice. "What are you doing here?"

He smiled weakly. "Surprise."

"Surprise for you, I'd say. Sorry I'm..." She waved a hand down her body.

Clint wondered if she knew how she looked. Her heavy blue terrycloth robe trailed its belt to the sides, and the dark purple flannel pajamas underneath might be a little saggy from over-wearing and under-washing. Fluff escaped from her deerskin slippers, and her matted brown hair could use a good brushing. Apparently winter had come early to Colorado and he'd interrupted her hibernation.

To his eye, she looked adorably pregnant. Which he would keep to himself. "I should have called. I did make a hotel reservation in case you weren't home, or had a picnic to go to, or were throwing a party."

She barked out a laugh. He had to smile at the idea.

"No parties." Rachel finished a cracker and started a third. "When do you leave?"

Words deserted him.

"No, no," she rushed in. "I don't mean you're unwelcome. You said you got a hotel room. When are you flying home?"

"Oh. I'm going to Little Tree tomorrow. My flight's at noon."

She sagged into the couch even farther.

"Gives me time after I land to drive to the ranch in time for dinner."

"Cancel the hotel tonight. Stay here."

He eyed her, feeling like a nuisance. "Are you sure?"

"You're right." She pulled herself to sitting upright and forced a smile, though it wobbled. "You don't want to be here, especially not with me like this. I meant there's no reason for you to stay in a hotel when I have a perfectly good—" She stopped, her body so suddenly still he grew alarmed.

"What? What's wrong?"

Rachel shook her head a tiny bit. "Nothing. Guest room.

Clean."

"Rachel?" He shifted to rise and go to her.

She put up a detaining hand like a traffic cop and he subsided into his seat, eyeing her closely.

"I'm fine. For a minute." She swallowed hard. "You're welcome to stay but I understand if you don't want to. I'm not exactly fun right now."

"I didn't come for fun."

She quirked a brow at him.

He grinned. "Not to say you aren't fun all the time."

"I meant sex. I probably won't be feeling like that today."

"And I can go without today. I came to see how you are."

"This is how I am." Her smirk turned into a soft smile. "It's weird, and maybe you're the only person who would understand this, but I kind of don't hate the sickness because it means I'm pregnant."

"Yes, you are." He understood perfectly.

"I am." Tears formed in her eyes. She jumped to her feet. "Oh crap."

He raced after her to the bathroom, reminding himself this was a normal phase. Little Bingo was making his or her presence known. It was, in a way, a positive thing, as she'd said.

He gathered up her hair as she vomited, dodging her waving arm trying to bat him out of the room. He breathed through his mouth and thought of projects at work. When she finished, he handed her a tissue.

Rachel cleaned up and sank to the floor with her back to the bathtub. She looked even paler, which he'd have deemed impossible. "Sorry. This isn't what you signed up for."

"This is *exactly* what I signed up for. I'm supposed to help you. Support you." He handed her some toilet paper to wipe her chin, fighting down a shudder of revulsion. Some dad he'd make if he couldn't stomach a little puke. "I'm kind of the reason you've got morning sickness, after all."

She scowled at him. "Don't sound too proud of yourself."

He crowed, his mood swinging one-eighty. "Can't help it. I guess the caveman gene is swirling to the top. I'm propagating the species. It's a primal urge."

"Cocky bastard," she muttered.

He might have taken offense but right then he had to hold her hair while she threw up the last (he hoped) of the saltines.

Fortunately, Rachel couldn't see him in the mirror, as she might not appreciate his huge smile. A million emotions rolled through him. He felt bad she was puking, but that came with pregnancy, so it didn't worry him. Too much. He was thrilled she carried his child, and felt grateful she'd let him be here for her, given their odd relationship.

They wouldn't have sex, and he could admit his relief that the subject wouldn't come up again today. Her saying they wouldn't make love this trip didn't rule it out in the future. Or did it?

He had no idea if sex remained an option between them since…there was no "reason" to make love. They didn't have the kind of relationship that included sex now. They were merely friends with a common interest.

He'd done his part in that department. Now his job was to act as support and eventually a role model for the kid. Whatever Rachel needed.

Would she expect him to be in the delivery room? His head went light.

"Clint, are you all right?"

CHAPTER EIGHT

November

Rachel basked in the glow of having some of her family around her dinner table for Thanksgiving. She usually spent it with friends or made the rare trip to Little Tree if the weather forecast favored travel. Having Grace, Mike and two of his siblings, Anita and Paul, over for a Thanksgiving Eve dinner meant the world to her. Tomorrow, Mike's family would gather and celebrate while Rachel ate leftovers and watched Hallmark movies. She couldn't think of a better way to celebrate the holiday.

Unless Clint could have joined her.

But she pushed away that thought. She couldn't expect more of him. He'd given her a baby, after all. The reminder of little Bingo made her smile and put a hand on her still-flat abdomen. "Are you sleeping in there, little one?" she whispered. "I guess you could be doing acrobatics. You're so tiny, I'd never feel it."

She couldn't wait to experience that first flutter of movement, and had to admit she'd be relieved when it came.

The books said to expect a butterfly sensation at around five months, along with starting to show an increased waistline. Next month, once she started showing, the time would come to tell the world.

Would the principal bring her before the education board as a poor role model? An unwed pregnant teacher didn't telecast "high moral conduct," as specified in her contract. Could she be suspended or put on unpaid leave? She'd have to re-check the wording before paranoia—and hormones—ruled her thoughts.

Whatever happened, she didn't regret her choice to become a mom. If they fired her, she'd move and find another teaching job. Nothing tied her to Longmont since her mom had passed four years ago.

Before dinner, she and Grace snuck upstairs for a little heart-to-heart when Anita insisted she and her brothers would warm up the meal. Rachel had prepared a few side dishes, and Mike and the kids had made a turkey at their other sister's house.

Ensconced in privacy, Grace peppered Rachel with questions about the baby, their respective health statuses, and finally asked after the donor. "Have you ever heard from him?"

"Yes. Although that's not in our agreement." Rachel thought over what they'd agreed on. It grew more fuzzy as the months passed. She just had to hold on to the idea of her and the baby alone together so she didn't get her heart broken.

She wasn't in love with Clint, so a broken heart? Not a chance. "He's being great, visiting more than I thought he would."

Grace raised a skeptical eyebrow as she eyed Rachel over her wineglass. "Then where is he? It's Thanksgiving, a day to be with your loved ones." Her mouth dropped. "He's not married, is he?"

Rachel laughed. "No. You don't understand donorship, do you? The guy offers his sperm, not his entire future. But to put your mind at rest, we did talk about him coming." *Before I knew you would be here.* "He has to work tomorrow. He couldn't even go home to visit his family—siblings, Grace. He doesn't have a wife."

"Girlfriend?"

"No. Although it isn't any of my business." Rachel tried to think of Clint as just a sperm donor. If she'd gone through *in vitro*, she wouldn't even have known what he looked like. "His obligation ended at the act of donation. That I have any kind of contact with him is unusual."

"Hmm." Grace sipped her wine, mind spinning so loudly Rachel could almost hear it. Rachel had opened the wine she'd bought for Grace and Mike over their protests, declaring it silly they should forego alcohol on her account. Mike's brother, Paul, she noted with relief, had declared himself the designated driver and opted for lemonade along with Anita. Grace had confided about Paul's adventures with alcohol and their worry for him.

"You're right," Grace said now. "It is weird that this guy's still hanging around."

Rachel drew back in surprise at this about-face. "What? Just a minute ago—"

"A minute ago, you hadn't made your feelings clear. I thought you wanted him here, but I can see he's bothering you."

"Bothering me? No. Not in the least. He's seriously great. A friend." Rachel paused for breath. "Why would you think otherwise?"

"You said it was unusual for him to be hanging around. He doesn't have a wife or girlfriend and he had to donate sperm to get any action."

Rachel laughed at the idea, still reeling from the picture Grace drew. "He's not like that. Believe me, he would have no problem finding a sex partner if that's all he wanted."

"Then why doesn't he?" Grace challenged. "What's he hanging around here for? I mean, no offense."

"Oh, not at all."

They sat with their own thoughts for a moment. Rachel didn't like hers. Why was Clint hanging around? They hadn't made love—had sex—the last few times he'd visited. They talked on the phone, and he asked about her and Bingo's health and Rachel's students. He called her in celebration when one of his photographs had been used in an ad campaign a colleague put together. Basically...

"He's become a friend. And he's a good guy. A caring, decent man. That's all the motive he has."

"Hmm. If you say so."

For the first time, Rachel wished she wasn't right. Having Clint as only a friend might be too bittersweet if she didn't keep her perspective. When the baby was born and he faded from their lives, she would have to deal with being alone again.

She needed to get her head straight. Donor. Friend. Cherished memory.

That, she could handle.

December

As she looked through the closet rack for her snowman sweatshirt, Rachel zipped her slacks and pulled together the tabs on the waistband, absently tugging. Spotting a black sleeve in the back she believed to be the one she sought, she pawed through the closet. Eureka. She usually waited until January to wear this, glad to have something festive after the holiday, but the snowfall last night called for warmth and cheer today. Kids had always responded well to the happy snowman, probably because it made them dream of having a snow day off school.

Looking out the window as her head emerged from the neckline, Rachel checked the inches of new snow on her street. She'd already cleared her driveway and walk with her snowblower. Nothing new had accumulated since then. She wouldn't mind a day off herself, but it looked like it wouldn't happen today. The kids would be rowdy, feeling cooped up. She felt a little restless too.

Rachel jammed her feet into hiking boots and checked her large tote bag for her street shoes, lunch, and the papers she'd graded the night before. All ready to go. The backseat of the car held a shovel, a scraper, a small bag of sand, and a blanket, as well as candles in a metal can, matches, a liter of water, and three chocolate bars. She'd probably make it the two miles to school.

Head down, Rachel kept one eye on the walk in case ice had formed since she blew the rest off earlier. Layers of outerwear blocked the sharp dry wind from slicing her skin open.

Fortunately, her car churned to life and she arrived at the school, chilled but unharmed. Rachel removed her crocheted scarf, hat, and mitten set from Lexi and put them on the shelf in her coat closet.

A rap of knuckles on her classroom doorjamb had her peeking around the closet door then stifling a silent groan.

Henry Lanigan waited, an expectant raise of his eyebrows giving her no clue as to what he wanted. Had she forgotten a meeting? He'd taught music last year, but they'd lost their funding for a full-time music program, so he'd been hired on for fourth grade this year. They often consulted on how her past students fared in his class or on his future ones now in hers, but she didn't recall anything on her calendar. "Good morning, Henry."

"Rachel." He gave a nod.

What had she ever seen in him and his imperious manner? He'd been a horrible choice of boyfriend. She couldn't imagine him as a donor. With a silent prayer of thanks to whatever forces had sent Clint to her, she swung off her coat and hung it up before turning back to Henry.

"I thought you might be in earlier today."

"Why?" When he didn't answer, she tried to be reasonable. The school had a zero tolerance policy for name-calling, so she kept thoughts like *jerk* and *pompous ass* to herself. "Did you need something?"

"The third grade evaluations are due."

"Not until after the holidays. If I recall, they're not due until January tenth."

"I hoped you might have them finished so I could review them over the break."

His tone implied she was slacking in her responsibilities

and inconveniencing him. She didn't need him to review them either. He represented the third-to-fifth grade teachers in some administrative meetings, but not all work had to pass through him. Rachel took a breath for patience. "I don't have them completed yet, but I will by the deadline."

"Hmm. I told Mr. Harrison I might have my report done when we returned from the break. I'll have to update him of this setback."

Tattling to the principal? She ground her teeth but replied, "It's not a setback as we'll meet our deadline. At least, *I* will."

His beady eyes narrowed, and she regretted baiting him.

"You usually wear that sweatshirt in January."

Rachel blinked, taken by surprise. Was it sweet her former boyfriend had noticed her clothing habits—or was it as creepy as it felt? "A snowman felt appropriate today. Why?"

"I thought you might have chosen it because it covers your waistline."

"My waistline?" She automatically checked for food stains but found her sweatshirt and gray slacks spotless.

"I know you like to indulge in sweets and carbs this time of year." He smiled as though she were a simpleton who couldn't curb her impulses.

She put a hand to her hip, too annoyed to hide her reaction. "I don't find your personal comments charming or appropriate, Henry. We're no longer dating, so if I eat a dozen pastries or gain a dozen pounds, it's no business of yours."

His gaze dipped to her waist before meeting hers again. "I don't know that you've gained a *dozen* pounds, Rachel, but it's rather early in the season not to be able to snap your pants, isn't it?"

He disappeared while she flipped up her sweatshirt. The jerk. He could have just said she'd forgotten to snap her pants. For Pete's sakes, she thought as she pulled the tab toward the hook. He could be quite a— She tugged. A pain in the— She bent to peer closer, trying to guide the tab.

Then it hit her. Her pants wouldn't close. Not because she'd indulged in sweets, but because she'd indulged in Clint.

She was *showing*.

She cupped a palm over her stomach as tears tickled her eyelids. She blinked, a huge smile settling goofily onto her face. "Hello, little one."

Rachel couldn't recall if the baby was supposed to kick before she started "increasing," and she tried not to worry. Surely nothing had gone wrong. Even if the books said she should feel Bingo kick first, she'd force herself to mark it down to individuality. A "your mileage may vary" kind of thing.

Happily, she noted her zipper had advanced to the top, and as her jerky ex pointed out, her sweatshirt would cover her gaping waistband.

Her overwhelming instinct was to call Clint. And say…what? I'm too fat for my clothes? I've gained a pound or an inch—a couple probably, to cause this problem—around my middle. He'd think she'd gone nuts. Or eaten too many "sweets and carbs."

No, Clint was neither pompous nor a jerk. He'd be happy for her.

For her. Not for them.

She decided to keep this development to herself. To cherish this newest sign of little Bingo, and rejoice that it meant her baby was growing.

Rachel closed the hallway door so no one would intrude on her private joy. Or hear her giggling. Or see her wiping away tears of gratitude as she improvised fastening her slacks with a rubber band.

She'd have to buy some maternity pants. Later, she might be horrified at the choices, but now, the idea was just one more thing to make her smile.

Clint cheered when his niece's ball of Christmas gift wrap landed in the recycle bag. "Two points."

Anna took a bow. Last year, she'd been jumpy and eager to move on to the next present. Seeing her growth over the past months both warmed his heart and chilled him to the bone. His child, Rachel's child, would grow up just as fast, an infant one moment and a bounding toddler the next. He'd miss the changes, the important milestones, and the small moments.

"Think fast," Jack said.

Clint looked up, years of being the younger brother coming to the rescue. He raised a hand reflexively and batted at a wad of wrapping paper right before it hit his face. His rebound flew toward the Christmas tree, narrowly missing an antique glass ball.

"Children," Lexi remonstrated.

He grinned and pointed at Jack. "He started it."

"You looked a million miles away," Jack replied. "I was just getting your mind off work and back to the family."

Lexi shook her head.

"Might as well give up," Uncle Crusty advised Lexi. "I done my best raisin' them two hellions, but manners just never took."

Clint and Jack burst into laughter. Crusty had been the rowdiest hellion in Little Tree—maybe in the entire state of Montana. He'd become their guardian only when the boys hit their early teens. Any manners had been instilled by their folks before their deaths. Crusty had focused on them working hard on the cattle ranch. His sagest parental advice had been "don't get caught."

"Sorry, Lexi," Clint said. "If you could control your husband, maybe he'd finally get to move off the Naughty list."

Jack leaned over and kissed her cheek. He looked into her eyes as he said, "Where's the fun in that?"

She blushed, and Clint turned away. There wouldn't be any kind of intimacy like that in his future with Rachel. If he had any future with Rachel. Their relationship lacked rules.

He held his breath as Jack opened the picture of Marco's Miracle Clint had photographed in June and framed. After adjusting the lighting and playing with angles, Clint regarded the photo as one of his best. The colt had been conceived after Jack's favorite stallion was gelded, a long shot of nature, hence his name.

Jack held the picture, showing no expression, and Clint's stomach knotted. He didn't doubt his abilities, but maybe Jack would have preferred a picture of Lexi or Anna or even Marco. Or Crusty.

"This is..." Jack looked up and the wonder on his face allowed Clint to take a breath. "Perfect."

Crusty grunted approval while Lexi and Anna enthused over the gift with sufficient superlatives to reassure him, but he didn't need to hear them. Jack's expression and one word summation bolstered his confidence as an artist.

Clint had taken other pictures on his visits home and several of them were under consideration for advertising campaigns. He'd wait until confirmation of the sales to tell his family. Getting his name known as a photographer would be the first step to a freelance career, something he'd been working toward for over a year. The money wouldn't hurt either, but the main coup would be to make the contacts. Then he'd have the money to quit his job and freelance, or maybe work part-time on commercial projects, so he could concentrate on landscape photography.

The change wouldn't happen overnight, but enough people had encouraged his talent that he believed he could do it. He'd been restless for a while now. He'd thought Montana had been calling him home—until he met Rachel. Maybe the state had called him home so he could meet her and fulfill the next part of his destiny.

Fatherhood.

Twenty-five seemed like the perfect age to settle down. It felt like a milestone of sorts, and in a month, he'd have another birthday. He'd grown tired of dating, of being alone, of his job, and he hated being dissatisfied yet not knowing what to do about it. Time was a-wastin', as Crusty would say.

While Crusty and Anna tackled cleanup, with the old man supervising from his recliner, Clint snuck to his bedroom to call Rachel. An overpowering need to make the connection pulled at his gut. He texted her first. MERRY CHRISTMAS! CAN WE FACETIME?

The icon for her FaceTime came up and he swiped a hand through his hair in lieu of a comb then answered. "That was fast. I wasn't sure you were available."

"I am. Merry Christmas."

He returned the greeting, soaking in her beauty. The last time he'd seen her in person, she'd had morning sickness. Their communications since had been non-visual. "You're looking good. We just finished opening presents."

"Oh." Her face fell even as she smiled. "I miss everyone so much. Tell them I said hi."

"Uh… How would explain talking to you?"

"Oh, right. I forgot. They don't know we know each other. Not more than meeting at the wedding. You're off somewhere private where you can talk, right?"

A thought knocked him sideways and his heart pounded so hard and fast with excitement he figured she could hear it in Colorado. "Unless you're ready to tell them about us? I mean, about Bingo. It'd be a great Christmas surprise for everyone." He held his hope in check.

"I hadn't thought of telling anyone. Not yet."

Disappointment seized him but Clint held his expression neutral. Or so he hoped. "You want to wait, huh?"

"Yeah. I haven't felt the baby kick yet and it's five months already."

He swallowed. Was that a bad sign?

"That doesn't mean anything's wrong," she rushed on. "As a matter of fact, I'm showing. Not much, but it means the baby is growing."

Joy nearly made him speechless. "What?"

She giggled. "Yeah. I know. It's really real."

"I have to see it. Show me."

She shook her head quickly with a giggle. "No."

"You have to. I want proof the baby's all right."

Her expression softened. "He or she is fine."

"Rach, come on."

"There's not much to show." But the phone picture jiggled as she maneuvered around, presumably undoing her clothes off-screen. "I bought myself a pair of maternity pants for Christmas."

Dammit. He should have thought of that. He'd sent her a photo album of the Grace-Jack-Lexi wedding weekend when they'd met and a landscape of the Rockies he'd taken in the national park near her. Now he considered it a stupid gift, as she saw the mountains every day.

"Okay," she said on a huff of breath. "Ready to be dazzled by my baby bump?"

"Dazzle away."

The video traveled quickly down to her abdomen. He could see her soft flesh and belly button, but it didn't appear any different than the last time he'd seen her naked. Which he must not think about now.

"Are you dazzled?" came her voice off-camera.

"Absolutely," he lied. "Give me that profile shot again."

The camera moved dizzily in, out and around. Maybe there could be a trace of a shadow indicating a slight mound.

Her face came back in view. "You're not seeing it?"

"A little. I think."

Her expression fell. "Oh."

"I'm sorry, Rachel. You're just not fat."

She laughed. "I will be though. A few days ago, I had trouble with" —she grimaced— "buttoning my pants."

"And that upsets you?" He would have thought she'd be happy. Another sign Bingo thrived in her womb.

"No, but a colleague saw me with my snap undone. Okay, my ex-boyfriend. And he said something about me overindulging in sweets." She shrugged. "I would rather he hadn't been around when I realized my pants didn't close."

So would Clint. His back teeth gnashed together.

"But he left and I had a moment alone with the baby before the students came in."

"You work with your ex?"

"What? Oh. Yeah. He teaches fourth grade, so I have to see him too often."

At least she sounded peeved. Had this guy been a prospective sperm donor at some point? Clint shook off the thought. If he had been, he'd missed out. *That baby is mine.* "Maybe I can swing by for New Year's. See that bump myself."

"Do you have time off?"

He didn't. He had two days for the holiday, the same as Christmas.

"That's a sweet thought," Rachel said, obviously reading the answer on his face. "But I won't be any bigger in a week. Let's wait. Maybe the next time we talk, I'll have something to show. What's going on at work? Any exciting projects?"

He didn't like the way she rushed past setting a date for his visit. Was she pulling away? Was this a hormonal thing, protecting the baby from others? Was this what the books called nesting?

Except, he wasn't "others."

Frustrated, he filled her in on the freelance prospects he had out for consideration.

"I'd wish you luck," Rachel said, "but I'm sure your talent will carry the day and you won't need luck. I'm going to try to make a baby blanket. I figure I have two weeks of vacation to get the top done. Then I can quilt it during the winter, a bit at a time."

She talked about a book she also planned to read and TV shows she wanted to binge over the holiday break. As she talked about her solitary pursuits, he felt pushed further away. He yearned to get closer, and she needed him less.

While they said their goodbyes, Clint's focus re-centered

to ways he could be more useful to Rachel. The physical distance between them created emotional distance as well.

At least on her part.

CHAPTER NINE

January

Rachel sighed as she finished her sandwich at her desk. The teacher's lounge held no appeal with her colleagues discussing their exciting holiday trips they'd taken or complaining about the students' lack of joy being back at school. Eating at her desk gave her enough privacy to write out To-Do lists about the baby, but today her mind wandered.

She put a hand to her stomach, and another to her mouth to cover her burp. Must have eaten too fast. She'd felt a bit of gas yesterday at home too, after dinner when she settled down to finish piecing together her quilt top. It didn't look bad, and thank heavens, it was only crib size. Finishing might be possible before the baby came.

No burp came and the gassy bubble dissipated. She had to remember to take her food slowly. She had ten minutes till the kids returned from their lunch.

The bubble formed again, and Rachel stilled.

The baby. She cupped a hand over her abdomen, looking

at it in wonder. Her little boy or girl rolled around inside her, stretching and growing. Already pushing boundaries. She smiled, tears pricking her eyes.

"Hello there," she said softly.

The subtle brush felt like butterfly wings. Fleeting, soft, almost imperceptible. Regret swamped her. "I'm sorry I didn't recognize you yesterday. That was you, right? Hi. I'm your mommy."

Mommy.

Tears slid down her cheeks right onto her stomach.

She wiped them off. "That teardrop was me being silly, even though I know you can't feel it. Since you're going to find out anyway, I might as well tell you." She rubbed a hand on her tiny bump. "I'm the sentimental sort. My tears might mean I'm happy. Because I am. Oh, I am."

Backhanding the teardrops from her cheeks, she sniffled. She had to tell someone. This was too big and important a moment to keep to herself.

Grace. She'd call her cousin since Grace knew about the baby.

Rachel dug her phone out of her purse in the supply closet. Staring at her Contacts, she swallowed her nerves and pressed the right buttons. Waiting for the call to connect, she settled her hand protectively on her bump. Seconds ticked along. Finally, the ring on the other end stopped mid-tone.

"The baby kicked."

"What?" Clint's voice erupted with joy. "Oh my God, Rachel, that's great! What's it feel like?"

No way would she say gas. That wouldn't be accurate anyway. "Like the fluttering of butterfly wings inside me."

He laughed. "Wow. That must be incredible."

"It is." She wiped away more happy tears. "He kicked yesterday but I didn't recognize it. I'm the worst mommy ever."

"This is your first pregnancy. No one would expect you to know what movement feels like."

"Thank you for saying that. I have to go; the kids are due back from lunch in a minute. But I had to call. I had to tell someone."

"I'm glad you did."

She frowned. "I don't think that's true."

"Yes, it is. I'm extremely glad you called."

"No, no. I believe you. I'm calling myself a liar. Clint, I had to call *you*. I had to tell *you*. No one else."

"Well, I'm still glad. But who else would you tell?"

"Grace. I thought I was going to call her. Picked up my phone. Then I pulled up your number. Clint, I wanted to share this with you."

A moment of silence made her wonder if she'd overstepped. Didn't he want to know about the milestones the baby achieved?

She backpedaled. "At Christmas, you were curious about the bump showing, so I thought—"

"No, no. Rachel." He took an audible breath. "I'm honored that you called me, that you wanted to share this moment with me. It's a big deal. Thank you."

Her shoulders slumped as she relaxed. "Phew. I never know what to tell you."

"Everything." His emphasis on the one word gave it impact.

Rachel smiled through more tears. "Then I will."

"Thanks for calling."

"I hope I didn't interrupt your work. I'm not actually sure what you do."

"I'm in a meeting of high-powered execs. This could cost me my job."

She laughed and said her goodbyes.

"Sorry," Clint told the others at the table as he returned to the room. "Did I miss anything?"

His boss shook his head. "We decided about your photograph, about using it in the ad campaign. Or not."

Clint's heart thudded but he tried to keep it casual. He slid into the chair he'd abandoned on seeing Rachel's name on Caller ID. Maybe no one would notice his knees had given out. The double whammies—baby kicking and decision time—

made him breathless. This could be the start of his freelance career and his bid for freedom.

"So what's the verdict?"

Rachel caught herself smiling all day. The baby hadn't kicked again, or she hadn't felt it, but just knowing her baby moved made her giddy. She would enjoy the moment, since she'd read about the later discomfort she'd experience. Nothing could ruin this feeling of joy.

By the end of the day, she was counting the hours till the weekend. The school board would probably frown if she tied every rowdy child to a chair or duct taped every mouth in the room. Probably. Many board members were former teachers and would sympathize. Doubtful she'd get away with it, though.

So she took a moment during their—unfortunately—indoor recess, since new snow had dropped another inch outside. Which was nuts since the kids couldn't wait for school to be over to go play in the snow. After marching the kids around the room to a song and setting classical music on low, she set out baby carrots to snack on and let the kids pick out books for a quiet break. Stepping into the hall, she leaned her head back on the wall and just breathed.

The baby kicked. She imagined him giving her a high five on a job well done. With a tender smile, she cupped her tiny bump.

"Oh my God." Henry's voice broke into her happy space.

She turned to find he'd advanced within feet and was studying her like an unidentified lab specimen.

"You went and did it. You actually did it."

Rachel pushed away panic and sought for calming thoughts. He could make trouble. He would delight in it.

"Yes, Henry. I told you my plans," she said quietly, hoping he would match her lower tone.

"But I didn't think you would go through with it." At least he'd dropped his voice to a hiss. "I mean, after I said no, and we broke up, I thought you'd drop this…this plan of yours."

As though I needed your permission? Like I couldn't do it without your help?

She took a breath. "I thought we were close enough to trust you with my plan to have a baby. Even once you didn't want to help me conceive" —thank God— "I thought you understood I was going to do it anyway."

His face darkened with disgust. "So how'd you do it? I mean, with who? Some guy you met in a bar?"

She clenched her teeth against the insult and the urge to spit back. "I have standards. That's why I asked you in the first place. We were close. I believed we might have been on the way to something permanent."

But you were too big a jerk. Fortunately, she hadn't tied

herself to him. His attitude was one reason she'd opted toward clinical donation. A test tube didn't have opinions. "Fortunately, I found a man who was happy to help."

Henry narrowed his eyes, looking her up and down. "I bet."

She took another breath, determined not to be baited. "You didn't want to help, and you didn't want to stay with me, so you can't be upset now. Isn't that a bit 'dog in the manger?'"

"Consider the example you're setting for the children. The school board won't like this."

Bile rose to the back of her throat. It would serve him right if she threw up right on his shoes. "I'm not doing anything wrong."

"You're an unwed mother."

She couldn't hold back a smile. "Yes, I am."

Henry gave a growl of frustration, probably holding back swear words in the school setting. "We'll see if you're still smiling after the news gets out."

"Would you seriously go to the school board?" Her words were brave, but she shook. "It's not the 1950s."

He sneered. "Oh, I know a lot of parents who won't view this moral issue as old-fashioned. Influential people in the district."

"Henry," she called quietly to stop him from walking

away with the last word. "Everyone knows we used to date. You don't want this to look like sour grapes."

"What do you mean?"

"Like you're mad someone else could do what you couldn't."

She let that stew for a moment and saw when he got her meaning. His face turned purple with anger, his body went rigid, and his hands tightened. This time he didn't suppress the swear word.

She couldn't have cared less.

On the other side of the security line, Clint scanned every face for Rachel's. He hadn't wanted her to fly, but she'd been determined to do "one last thing" before her doctor grounded her. Despite his misgivings, he was excited she'd made the effort to come see him. Perhaps exchanging the snow of late January in Colorado for the sun and relative warmth of L.A. had been a draw, but he wanted to think his presence had been an incentive as well.

As they both had a long weekend holiday for Martin Luther King Day, three days stretched before them. He wished she'd been able to fly out earlier, but she'd had an in-service teacher meeting that morning. He'd been able to clear his desk for the weekend. They'd have two and a half days together, given she'd fly home on Monday at noon. He intended to make the most of it.

Finally, Rachel rounded the corner. He drank in her face while still unobserved by her, not wanting to be a jerk. She had a large tote on her shoulder, a winter coat over her arm, and pulled a rolling carry-on bag. He smiled, wondering how long she planned to stay after all.

Rushing to her side, he tried to see any sign of his child inside her but couldn't. She'd said Bingo was just a small bump, but he'd hoped for evidence of its existence. Last time he'd seen her in person, she'd been going through morning sickness and looked pale. Except when she turned green and threw up. He determined not to let this much time pass between visits again. Not sure how he'd pull it off, he'd have to think on it this weekend.

She saw him and broke into a smile, quickening her pace. Not letting doubts or second thoughts hinder him, he swept her into a hug. "Just friends" be damned.

"Rachel, you look great. How was the flight?"

"Good. It's so warm here." She kissed his cheek then glanced around. "Which way to baggage claim?"

He had to laugh. "You have more stuff?"

She made a face at him. "Maternity clothes are bigger."

Taking the tote bag from her shoulder, he said, "Give me the roller. We have to take the escalator."

"I can manage."

He took the luggage handle from her fingers. "You need a free hand for the rail, and you're already carrying a coat."

She raised her brows. "If you think I'm touching that handrail, you're crazy."

"You have to hold on or you might fall."

"It's a rolling, rubber, germ factory."

Clint thought about all the people who touched the escalator rail on a given rotation. Looking around at the steaming, sweating throng of humanity in their different states of health and cleanliness, he had to agree. "Good point. I'll get on first and you can hold on to my shoulder."

"I'm not having any trouble with my balance. Yet."

"Humor me?"

She eyed him. "I feel this is a mistake."

"Using me for balance?"

"Giving in to you. This is not the beginning of a pattern, Clint Walker. This is a compromise to get my vacation started."

He was wise enough to swallow back a victorious smile.

On the ride to his apartment, Rachel gawked at everything they passed. Clint mostly saw palm trees and cars, but she noticed the oddities. Dogs dressed as though for Halloween, who had to be sweltering in their sweaters and party dresses in the sixty-seven degree heat. Their owners often dressed equally as strangely. She didn't exactly hang her head out the side of the car or point at every passing sight, but close. Half an hour in the city and she was already having fun. Her enjoyment pleased and enchanted him.

"The colors are mesmerizing. Everything at home is bland or white right now." She sighed and sailed her hand on the wind out the open window. "And I can't believe how warm it is."

"Enjoy it now. We'll get rain later."

"Rain? I thought it doesn't rain in southern California."

"We are in a drought." He smiled. "Except when it pours."

"Ha. That's right, isn't it?" She hummed a little of the classic song. "Well, as long as it's not three feet of snow, I'll manage. In that bag you teased me about, I have gear for all kinds of weather."

He pretended to be affronted. "I did not tease you."

"You asked whether I'd packed my bags intending to stay long enough to deliver the baby here."

"It's a legitimate concern. I would have a lot to prepare."

"Right. Anyway, I don't plan to be stuck inside because I'm *not* prepared."

"What do you want to do? Is there something in particular you'd like to see?"

"Is it too far to the beach?"

"Which one?"

"The one by the ocean." She rested her head back and smiled. "I don't know anything about the best place to do it. I just want to dip my toes in the Pacific."

"I think that can be arranged."

"Tomorrow. But as for right now? The baby is *starving*. Take me to your favorite place. Nearby."

"Your wish is my command."

"Oh, Clint, honey, you're going to regret saying that."

Her grin made him feel like the canary about to be eaten by the cat. He didn't mind that idea at all.

Rachel made a piece of toast and wandered Clint's apartment. He'd left a note saying he'd gone for a run. If he'd had sex with her, she thought sourly, he wouldn't have any excess energy to run off. But he'd put her in his bedroom and he'd slept on a pullout couch in his home office. While she appreciated his thoughtfulness...

Oh hell. She might as well be honest with herself. His hands-off policy ticked her off. The morning sickness had passed and she finally felt some energy. And frankly, she felt the itch to be with him too. Not just sex, and not just anyone. Sex with Clint. Couldn't she have one last hurrah before she was too fat and sloppy—and busy with the baby—to arouse interest in a guy?

She didn't want to pin a label on her need for intimacy

with him. Part of coming to L.A. had been to bolster her ego after Henry's comments. Part had been to have a break from winter and do something fun before she physically couldn't. Before she was—happily—tied to a baby and her home. One last time before the baby came and Clint faced the reality of her with no sleep and sticky clothes and a house full of toys and diapers. Once the baby was safely delivered, he'd realize his part was over.

Maybe his impending departure from her life had provided the strongest incentive for the trip, to see Clint. Video chatting only satisfied part of her need. He was fun, thoughtful, handsome, and interesting. She wanted to touch him, be held by him.

Have sex with him.

Growling her frustration, she read the titles of the books on his shelves. A fair number of them were mysteries and thrillers. Some general fiction and adventures. Nature and photography as she'd expected. More biographies than she'd ever read, from actors to zoologists. His history collection inspired envy. She'd definitely not be bored if they stayed in and read the weekend away.

Taking a history of horse soldiers to the couch, she settled in to the plush comfort. She'd pictured him with a black leather sofa, a huge TV, and glass accents. Sleek and L.A.-looking. While he had a tan leather couch, his coffee table and side tables were made of a rich wood, well polished. Wood featured in his bedroom, headboard and dresser, as well. A touch of the outdoors to remind him of Montana?

On his coffee table lay well-perused copies of two popular baby books. He'd been so sweet to get them for her. He must have gone to a used book store, as the spine was broken on one and the pages dog-eared on both. Still, they looked clean and otherwise almost new.

The lock turned and Clint stepped in with white bakery bags. Her attention perked up immediately.

"Hey." She rose to help him take the three bags to the kitchen counter. "Does your daily run justify this treat?"

He frowned. "I don't run."

She looked him over. A navy tee, jeans, and what looked like his cowboy boots. Scrumptious. "Your note said you went for a run."

"I meant donut run."

Rachel looked at the note on the kitchen counter again. He'd drawn a circle in a circle. Sure. She shook her head. Why hadn't she figured it out? She'd thought he meant he'd do a lap. Run around the block. Of those options, donuts won.

"But then I saw these." He placed fruit Danish on a plate. Strawberry and probably apricot. "And these." From another bag, he drew out muffins. Her mouth watered at the scents of cinnamon and spices. Her knees went weak when the pineapple-nut emerged, trailing sugar on the marble counter. She wet her finger and took care of those granules.

He might just be her favorite person, and she hadn't seen the contents of the third bag yet.

"I have fresh whole milk, two percent, and skim. And almond and soy milk. I wasn't sure what you're drinking these days. If the doctor recommended something in particular."

"I'm a skim milk drinker usually, but I've 'bumped' it up to two percent for the baby."

He smiled at her emphasis. "Some bump."

"It's getting more pronounced. And this breakfast will push it some more." She opened his cabinets and found glasses.

"I can make coffee."

Rachel grimaced. "I'm off caffeine."

"Okay. Good to know. Fortunately, California is the state of freshly-grown fruit, so we won't have any problem feeding you this weekend."

She sank her teeth into a Danish and found it to be lemon custard. Tangy and sweet flavors exploded on her tongue. She swallowed, wondering if she could cut off a tiny bite of each. "This is exquisite."

He chuckled. "I'll tell the bakery next time I'm there."

"Tomorrow?"

"This afternoon, by the looks of things."

She wrinkled her nose at him. "Can I help it if you're a

good provider? Uh, of snacks. Breakfast."

Crap. She didn't want him to think she expected anything from him long-term. She knew better. He wasn't staying. She tried again.

"For fulfilling my desires? Pandering to my needs?" It didn't come out as sexy as she'd have liked, but he faltered and she guessed the change of tact had distracted him from her stay-with-me-forever terminology.

He leaned close and whispered, "I haven't even shown you all the options."

He held the third bag under her nose and opened it. Chocolate cake donuts with chocolate icing.

The man really did understand her needs.

They spent the late morning into afternoon at the beach, dozing in the sun and walking along the hard-packed sand. Clint snapped picture after picture, more for memory's sake than a plan to do anything with them. Although... One view of Rachel from the back featured the ocean, and the pretty woman splashing in the waves didn't hurt any. The tourism board might buy it. Rachel delighted in the waves on her toes, but the chilly temperature had made her shriek with shock.

He took her to a Mexican/Thai/Greek restaurant just to make her laugh. She took a while deciding over the menu then declared everything "excellent," charming the waitress and the owner. When they returned to the apartment, Rachel fell asleep on the couch, in the middle of telling a story. Without waking her, he slipped the glass of water from her hand and put it on the coffee table.

She woke half an hour later while he sat nearby tinkering with the photos he'd taken earlier.

"Hey, that's me." Rachel leaned in over his shoulder, smelling of coconut sunscreen, strawberry shampoo and sunshine. "But you've done something. Changed it."

"A little bit. I thought I could sell it to a travel site, if that's okay with you."

"What? Sure."

"You'll have to sign a release. Whoever I sell it to will want to see one before they'll use the photo."

A furrow on her forehead accompanied her smile. "Not a problem. You can't see my face anyway. You'd said some of your photos were being featured in ads. Are you still enjoying that, like commercial photography instead of whatever you'd call it? I don't want to say 'instead of artistic' because I'm sure your stuff is artistic as well as money-making."

He laughed as she tried to cover her bases and not hurt his feelings. "I do enjoy it. Seeing my work used to convey an idea or emotion is pretty heady stuff. And I'm starting to see images, like you on the beach today, and immediately translate them into how they could be used and who might be a buyer.

Like a travel site, airline, tourist bureau, and so on. If Bingo had rounded you out more, I could have sold the shot to accompany an article on 'healthy pregnant living' or something."

She nodded. "Trust me, my hips are plenty wide. But since my face—and stomach—don't show, I could be anyone. It will appeal to more age groups."

Clint didn't agree. Rachel had a unique way of standing, turning her head, or even walking. She laughed like no one else, whether it came from her belly or trickled out as a giggle. But he couldn't say any of that without sounding like a sap.

Instead, he took a different chance. "My boss lined me up to freelance with a guy that opened a restaurant serving all natural, locally-sourced food, and I shot the photos for their brochures and website. The owner intends to change images regularly to keep things fresh-looking, and put me on retainer. I've sold well enough other places already and made multiple contacts that I've talked to my boss about working part-time. From home."

Her face lit. "That's great, Clint. Does part-time at your current job give you camera time?"

"That's the plan. And" —he paused for courage— "I can work from anywhere. Even Colorado."

She stumbled back a step, face suddenly white and expression slack. It took a moment for her to make words, and the effort showed. He waited on edge, and as the moment stretched out, he grew increasingly sure that edge of ground he teetered on would crumble beneath his feet.

"Colorado?" she squeaked.

"Yes. I said I'd help with the baby and be a role model as Bingo grew up."

"Well, yeah, you did. But…"

He waited.

And waited.

Until he couldn't. "But what?"

He couldn't read her expression. Or rather, her non-expression. She'd shut down, gone neutral.

"I thought that was all…you know. A thing one says."

Despite the serious natural of their discussion, he had to bite back a smile at her formality. "When does one say a thing like that?"

She squinted in displeasure at his teasing. "When one is trying to get in someone else's pants. With his donated sperm."

A laugh burst from him. "Oh. Right. *Then*. Happens all the time, I'm sure." He sobered. "Rachel, I've never donated sperm before. I haven't made promises to a woman for anything long-term since I kissed Carrie Moore in second grade and said I'd be her boyfriend forever."

"So you're taken?"

He shook his head. "She pushed me off the slide the next

week, said she didn't like me anymore and to never kiss her again."

"Ouch."

"Right. My dad was sympathetic about my scraped up hand and broken heart, but Crusty laughed his butt off. Point being, I'm not one to make promises lightly. Or break them."

He thought of Sheryl and how his refusal to make a promise had destroyed their relationship. If he'd married her and started the family she'd been desperate to have, she wouldn't have gotten pregnant by a stranger. If he'd been able to forgive her infidelity as a reckless mistake, she wouldn't have jumped in the car, tears blinding her. She wouldn't have wrecked. She wouldn't have endured the injuries that hooked her on oxy. She wouldn't have lost her ability to bear a child.

"So you're moving to Colorado?"

He nodded, letting Rachel adjust to the idea of him being in her state before he reminded her of the rest.

"Are you moving to Denver? Lots of advertising possibilities there, I bet."

"I'll be in a position to freelance on the Internet. I can set up a home office with a lot of my work still being sold to businesses here in L.A." He took a breath. "So I can live in Longmont. Be closer to you and Bingo."

"Stop calling him that."

"You do."

Rachel smiled and shrugged. "Rarely. And just to avoid saying 'he,' 'she,' or 'it.'"

Clint didn't argue. Or allow himself to be sidetracked. "And as long as I'm going to be in Longmont, and since I don't have anywhere else to live yet…"

Her eyes went wide.

"And since you're going to need help for the first months after the baby's born…"

Her mouth dropped open for a second before she recovered her voice. "You want to move in with me?"

He grinned. "Thanks. That'd be great."

Rachel's laugh surprised even her. "You are incorrigible."

"I'll start packing." Clint jumped up and hurried toward his bedroom.

She watched his retreat, reeling in disbelief. Surely he didn't think the matter resolved?

Her practical side agreed she'd need help for the first weeks or maybe up to a month after the baby came. The baby's world would narrow to sleep, food, clean diapers, and the physical comfort of being held. Rachel had read about moms being deprived of sleep, food, and the physical comfort of a bath. Or even a quick shower. Having help made sense.

But Clint providing it?

She knew he wanted to move back to Little Tree, to be closer to his family. Maybe Longmont would serve as the first stop on his journey home. He'd enjoy the baby-cuddling part, and maybe the feeding part, and she'd be sure he got acquainted with the diaper-changing part. His interest in the baby seemed sincere.

He'd probably be a great help, running errands and so on, until the glow wore off. Until he didn't get any sleep. Until the baby cried non-stop from colic, and the laundry piled up, and *his* laundry piled up. Then he'd sidle off like her dad, the reality not as fun as he'd hoped. In her dad's case, there'd been no son to carry his name and too many bills to pay. In Clint's case, he'd soon come to the conviction she could manage without him.

So she would. She'd treat his moving in as a visit. A long visit. And then he'd be free to go.

And if she kept reminding herself she'd soon only run into him at Lexi's family parties, she'd be fine.

"Clint. Can you come out here please?"

He returned, not a hesitation in his body.

"I've decided. You can move in. Stay until the baby's a month old, and then we'll see how your job is going." She made herself smile as though the thought of him leaving didn't break her heart. When had that become a possibility? "You might find you need to be here in L.A., or somewhere else, to network, make connections to get jobs. Or that you'd prefer 'working from home' to mean from Little Tree."

He opened his mouth. She couldn't bear to hear promises he'd later break. To set any hopes on him.

"So," she rushed on, "we have to decide when to tell the families."

"What?"

She'd successfully sidetracked him. "When to tell them I'm pregnant for starters. I can't just pop out a baby and not tell my cousins and uncle. And their first question is going to be 'who's the father?'"

He blew out a breath. "Right. Of course."

"Do we tell them it's you?" Now she held her breath. Would he want to hide the truth to avoid conflict within the families?

His jaw clenched. "I am the father. Why wouldn't you want to tell them?"

"Calm down. I didn't say that. I wondered if you wanted everyone to know. I mean, it could be our secret."

"I'm the baby's father."

She loved to hear him say it. To claim little Bingo.

"Okay, when do we tell them? You'll have to explain why you're moving and why to Longmont."

"I hadn't gotten that far, but yeah. I guess when I make the move and job change official, I'll tell them. They'll wonder at the new address. Why I didn't move home."

"If you'd rather move to Montana…"

"Are you moving to Montana?" he countered.

"No, but you've said you miss home. You mentioned it when we met at the wedding. How you'd like to do landscape photography and move back."

"I thought Little Tree and my family were calling. Now I think I just wanted a change." He took her into his arms and set his cheek against her hair. "That's probably why the donor idea appealed so much. Helping you, of course, but making a baby. Part of me being part of the future."

Rachel thought back over everything she could remember him ever saying and realized every word had been about the baby.

Not her.

It shouldn't hurt. By the time he'd learned about the donor idea, they'd had sex a couple of times, which didn't constitute having a relationship exactly. His heart hadn't been involved and still wasn't.

But she was afraid, very afraid, hers was.

CHAPTER TEN

February 15

When Uncle Kevin called, Rachel snatched up the phone as though it contained candy. Or cookies. Or her beloved, abandoned caffeine.

They exchanged pleasantries while she bit back the urge to tell him about the baby. He'd understand. He'd be supportive. He'd even be happy for her. Probably.

But she'd agreed to tell everyone with Clint when he moved in next month. And she had to admit to a feeling of relief at not having to face the music if she was wrong about Uncle Kevin's reaction.

"Iris is here bugging me to get to the point." The grin in his tone rang through the phone. Rachel could hear a female voice giving him grief. Mrs. Browning, the librarian? They'd been together at the wedding, but... And Grace had told her they were dating, but... Although of course Uncle Kevin deserved happiness of his own... And with the twins married and living away from home, carrying on with their own families…

Rachel took a deep breath.

She would have to adjust to thinking of him with someone romantically. The cousins had always been generous enough with their dad, seeing as she didn't have one—or not one worth mentioning anyway. Dear old Dad might be out there somewhere or he might have drunk himself to oblivion years ago. He hadn't come when Mom died and Rachel hadn't had any idea how to contact him. Uncle Kevin had stood in for his brother all these years. Now he'd have a new person to focus his attention on.

Which he totally deserved. Rachel shook off her selfish reflections and put a smile into her voice. "What's that point she wants you to get to?"

"We're getting married."

The pit dropped out of her stomach and her skin turned clammy. So much for not being selfish.

"Wow. That's great." She shook herself. "Congratulations, Uncle Kevin. And tell Missus, uh, Iris how happy I am for her. She's getting a prize."

He laughed. "I'm the lucky one. She's put up with me for years."

"Waited a long time too," came the laughing reply in the background.

"Yeah, we've been seeing each other for a while now.

Well, I'm not making her wait any longer," he said. "The wedding's set for June."

"Wow. That's great." And really soon. The baby would be about two months old by then. Their first appearance in Little Tree. Would Clint be by there? It wasn't a Walker event, though the groom was his brother's father-in-law. As well as Clint's baby's great-uncle. Such a tangled web.

"We set the date for the end of the month so you'd be done with school by then. Can't have my wedding without all three of my girls there."

Tears pricked Rachel's eyes. She felt as small as a microbe. "Thanks."

"Hey, now. Are you crying?"

She was. "Happy tears."

A lie. He'd planned his wedding around her, not knowing she'd be on maternity leave. He'd called to tell her his big news, and she'd kept hers a secret for seven months, give or take a few weeks.

She looked at the calendar and realized the date. "You proposed yesterday, didn't you? On Valentine's Day."

Uncle Kevin chuckled. "Hedging my bets. I thought all the romance in the air might put Iris in a softer, more agreeable mood, and she might agree to take me on permanently."

"Well, it seems to have worked."

"I'll say. Now I have to find a way to be patient through

all this wedding planning before she makes an honest man out of me."

Iris said something in the background that made him laugh. "I've gotta go. I wanted to call and tell you our news. Iris says hello."

"Tell her hello for me. And congratulations. She's getting the best man I know."

Rachel ended the call and held the phone to her chest.

The best man. Clint had made that joke at Grace and Jack's failed wedding weekend. She'd fallen for him a little bit then, enough to go to bed with him the second night after meeting him. And the next night, when he'd come to her house looking for Grace. Every time they were together, she'd found more traits about him she liked.

She couldn't argue the point. Clint lived up to the title.

In a few weeks, he'd move in with her and they'd have to tell everyone about the baby. They'd have to explain they weren't a couple, despite the baby they'd conceived, and despite Clint living with her temporarily. They'd have to explain Clint would be moving on in a few months, once she recovered and he'd figured out his future career plans.

Fortunately, she had a month to come up with those explanations. And to prepare herself for the reality of life without Clint. Rachel put a hand to her sternum to rub away the ache, but she feared this pain would last longer than indigestion.

When her phone dinged a FaceTime notification the next day, Rachel hoped it would be Clint. He liked to see the baby's inch by inch growth, which tickled her. Being alone in this venture, she loved having him to talk to about the pregnancy, though she omitted the parts that might gross him out. Sometimes she wished he called about her, not only the baby, but he was always nice enough to ask about her job. More in the form of the work not being too much for the baby, but she couldn't complain. Exactly.

And who would she complain to?

She hadn't heard from him in a week. He was busy closing down his office in L.A., subletting his apartment, and making his clients and contacts aware of his continued availability.

She picked up the phone to read Uncle Kevin's name.

Her heart climbed into her throat. *Crap.* Panicked, she ran a hand over her hair, pinched some color into her cheeks, and propped the phone on some books atop the table, hiding her waistline and fuller breasts. Uncle Kevin wouldn't be looking for signs, but he was a vet, for Pete's sake. He knew what pregnancy symptoms looked like. Glancing at the nearby mirror, she checked that she didn't look obviously pregnant in that position, then connected the video call.

"Hey," she said in a too-chipper voice. She toned it down to a more natural one and tried again. "What's going on?"

"I talked to Grace last night. She said she spoke to you yesterday and I should call. So maybe I should ask *you* what's going on."

Rachel closed her eyes. Had Grace outed her? She wouldn't, would she? Well, yes, she would, if she thought it was in Rachel's best interests to have her dad's support.

She glanced into the camera, noting her own pale image in the corner.

"Rachel," Uncle Kevin said in a gentle voice. "Are you upset about me getting married?"

Her whole body slumped. "Oh."

Drat that Grace. But at least she hadn't spilled the bigger bag of beans. "I'm not at all. You know I'm happy for you, right?"

He smiled. "I don't doubt that. But you do realize it doesn't change our relationship, I hope."

"It will." The words slipped out and Rachel scrambled to pull them back. "I mean, it *should*. You'll have a new bride. A new center to your world. I wouldn't want it otherwise."

"I'll have a wife, yes. And you'll still be my third daughter."

Tears burned and she blinked rapidly to keep them from falling. Forget Clint—Uncle Kevin was the best man she would ever know.

"You're not going to be one iota less important to me, Rachel."

Tears slid down her face without permission. She wiped them away impatiently, but more followed. "I know."

Somewhere deep inside she knew he meant it. He wouldn't ever intentionally shut her out, but he would focus now on his future with Iris. Which he *should*, her mind and heart agreed. That was normal and expected between a husband and wife. And she didn't begrudge him his happiness. It simply meant he'd be less available. His time would be spoken for.

He'd be less *hers*.

"It's only separation anxiety." She tried to laugh it off.

"There's nothing to be anxious about. We're not separating." He paused and his dear, familiar face folded into concerned lines. "Is that was this is? Rachel, I'm not leaving you. I'm not pulling away. I'm not my brother, the idiot."

She laughed. Another rapid switch of emotions. Crying while happy, laughing while sad. "I know."

"Do you? Look, I'll tell you again and again until you understand. He never deserved you or your mom. He was always too irresponsible for a family, even before he started drinking."

Her mom had said much the same. Daddy was too young, too immature, too self-absorbed. Rachel had never believed her dad left because of her. She came to understand it was just the thing men did. Her mom's second husband left too, about the time Rachel had started to think of him as another dad. Even Uncle Kevin always had to return home. And Henry the jerk had broken off their relationship.

Clint would move out, and move on, when she and the baby settled into a positive routine. When he got his photography business started up and knew where he wanted to live, which she imagined would be Little Tree, not Longmont or even Denver. She was lucky to have had him this long honestly, and she knew that too.

"Ignore me," she said. "I haven't seen you in a while, and I'm a little" —*hormonal*— "homesick."

"I'll be here whenever you're available to visit. Your room is waiting."

Rachel nodded.

"It has been too long, though, you're right. Maybe I should come visit you."

"No!"

He drew back in surprise.

"I mean… I'm busy with school. We wouldn't be able to visit."

But his expression had turned curious. She could practically feel his gaze drilling into her through the airwaves. She tried again for a positive, though not-so-bright-it-looked-fake smile

"You do look pale. Are you working too hard?"

She grasped the excuse. "A little. The students are restless. Every time we get a good weather day, they think winter is over for good."

"Why don't you come up for spring break? Do you good to get away, see the girls, and get to know Iris."

"I can't."

"Sure you can. Spring is your favorite time of year here."

"Any season I'm there is my favorite." Oops. She hadn't meant to give him more ammo. "It's just not possible right now."

"Give me a good reason you can't come."

I'm expecting a baby. My donor daddy is from Little Tree. And we're not a couple, traditional or otherwise.

"Uncle Kevin, I miss you all, and I'd come if I could."

"Okay. This is your home too, so if you change your mind at the last minute, just come. With every female animal in five counties pregnant, I won't be going anywhere for a few months."

"Until your honeymoon," she teased. When his mouth dropped open, she shook her head in mock disappointment, selfishly glad of a topic to distract him. "*Tsk, tsk,* Uncle Kevin. Did you forget to plan your own honeymoon?"

They brainstormed destinations and ended the call on a

happy note. Rachel practiced her rhythmic breathing, which purportedly helped women endure the physical pain of birth. She would also use that technique to wade through the emotional pain of the change in Uncle Kevin's life. And the pain of Clint leaving.

She swiped a few more tears away, growling at herself in frustration. She needed a lot more practice.

March 15th

Clint stacked the last of his boxes in the basement of Rachel's home. His home now too.

He'd felt her watching his every trip inside and down the stairs, and sure enough, she stood in front of him now as he topped the last step. He gave her a questioning look, not sure why she hovered. Maybe she worried he'd break something. Having a man move in must feel strange.

"I don't have much," he said. "I took most of my clothes to a consignment store in L.A. Light-weight suits and beach stuff will sell better there."

Rachel nodded. "I hate for you not to have your things. There's room downstairs. The basement is only a laundry area. We could add some hanging racks and storage bins."

"I brought a few suits and enough light-weight clothes for summer. It's the warmer stuff I'll need to stock up on, to supplement what I keep for winter trips to Little Tree."

Her mouth opened though no sound emerged. She shook off whatever she'd been going to say.

"What is it?"

Rachel retreated to the kitchen. He followed, waiting while she poured him a lemonade. She handed him the glass of full of ice and bright yellow liquid, fresh-squeezed and a little sweet. "It's just…a lot of decisions awfully fast."

Clint perched on a chair in the kitchen and eyed her while he took another drink. He tried to assess her mood, to suss out her meaning. She looked… Damn beautiful. Rounded out to nearly bursting, she'd grown a little wide both side to side and front to back. Her skin glowed, and her eyes were bright with a spark of…well, *life* inside her.

He'd experienced barely a hitch moving to Longmont and moving in with Rachel, and had no doubts about the decision.

Except for the worried expression he often caught on her face before she smoothed it away. She claimed to be pain-free when he asked, and of course everything was "fine."

He set down the glass. "Is it fast though? We talked about me moving in when you visited in January. Have you not gotten used to the idea in the past months? The baby's coming, ready or not."

"No, I know. I'm ready."

"For the baby."

She nodded, gaze on her cup of chocolate milk. Her

fingers trailed around and around the rim. He remembered those fingers on him, making paths on his skin, and he shivered with longing.

But she was far too pregnant for any of that to happen. He changed the subject.

"My mom used to do that."

Rachel glanced up, surprised and distracted out of her pensive mood. "What?"

He indicated her mug. "Make rings on her glass. She didn't have a lot of free time, working on the Rocking W with Dad and Crusty, but she used to play songs. Not songs, exactly. High-pitched tones that she'd make up words to." He smiled in memory. "The dogs hated it. Jack used to cover his ears and run from the room, but as shrill as it sounded, I always loved her nonsense songs."

"I've never heard you tell a story about your mom."

"I don't guess it's come up." Clint shrugged. "We all worked out on the ranch most of the time. Boy, could she ride. Maybe even better than the men, although I didn't think anything of it at the time."

Rachel crossed her arms and leaned forward, her expression eager. "She enjoyed riding and working with the cattle and ranch hands?"

He settled in to the chair, happy to share stories about his family. "I never heard her complain about it."

"That's not the same thing, you know."

"She had a favorite horse, a chestnut gelding. Called him Apples because he gobbled them up from her hand. His real name was Apollo, and he was not only a beauty but strong. He could work all day and go for a pleasure ride in the moonlight."

Rachel looked wistful and he remembered he never took her for that ride last June. "Did that happen often?" she asked.

"The working sure did. Mom and Dad would ride off sometimes together for a private picnic instead of having dinner with us. I guess it was hard to be surrounded by men and work all the time."

"Probably. At least Lexi has Annabeth and your housekeeper to talk to."

Clint nodded. "Mom didn't seem to mind just having guys around. She had friends in town."

"No cowgirls working the range?" Rachel teased.

Clint scoffed at the idea. "With Crusty in charge?"

"Right."

"It might have been the turn of the twenty-first century, but that man's mind is stuck in the 1800s. You'll be happy to hear Lexi is chiseling away at that granite head of his. She's the only female he's more than tolerated since Mom died." He leaned close to confide, "I think he actually likes Lexi."

"No way."

"Don't quote me, but yeah, I think so."

"So he liked your mom?"

Clint had to smile. "One year, when I was about six, I asked him to take me to town. He scowled, of course. When I said I needed to go shopping, he looked sour enough to have been drinking rattlesnake juice."

"Is that a thing?"

"Shh, I'm telling a story."

Rachel giggled and nodded for him to continue.

"He said" —Clint put on a growly voice— "'what in tarnation fer and why do ya think I'd take ya?'"

She laughed. "What did you want to buy?"

"A present for my mom for Mother's Day. Well, when I told him that, all the starch went out of his backside."

"He agreed?"

"He grumbled and harrumphed a little, and said he guessed he was going into town later that day, and he could probably stand to have me along if I didn't plan to talk in the truck or take forever to make up my mind. I promised I wouldn't." He smiled again in memory. "I knew exactly what I wanted."

"What?"

"A little statue of a horse. Chestnut brown, broad chest."

"Aww, sweet."

"But…"

"Oh no. You couldn't afford it?"

"I sort of had the money. Crusty asked me that too. 'Ya gots any money saved?' I told him I'd been saving since I first saw the horse statue at the Feed Store. The old man's eyes went buggy, and he said, 'a horse statue?' like it was the most absurd thing ever."

"That's not nice."

"No one ever accused Crusty of being nice, even to little boys."

"So if you had the money, what was the problem?"

"It had been sold."

"No!"

Clint nodded. "I didn't know it was a piece of artwork. I thought it was like boots or hammers, that there'd be more in the back."

"And?"

"Crusty found out who'd made it, and he took me to where she worked at her day job. Pottery was her hobby. She was good. I think she could have made good money if we had a gallery and she wasn't selling out of the feed store."

"Clint. Get back to the story. Did she have another horse figurine you could buy for your mom?"

He shook his head.

"Oh." Rachel sank back in her chair.

"So Crusty shook his finger at her. 'Ya better git home and make one then. This boy wants to git it for his mom for

Mother's Day. That don't give you much time, and he wants a good-looking horse, not one just thrown together cuz ya think ya got a done deal.'" Clint shook his head. "I was mortified. I wanted to crawl under the desk and hide."

"What did she say?"

"'Shhh.'"

"Tell me."

"No, I mean that's what she said. Shhh. Because, after all, we were in the library."

Rachel's eyes went wide with realization. "No way."

He nodded. "Mrs. Browning."

"Uncle Kevin's Mrs. Browning? She does pottery?"

"She did."

"Well, I'll be darned. I keep forgetting what a small town Little Tree is."

"Smaller back then if you can believe it."

"I was there, at least for some summers. Get back to the story. Did she make a figurine for you?"

He nodded.

"Did your mom love it? Of course she did. It was a present from her little boy."

"Yeah. I got major points. Mom made a big deal out of Jack's present too, but his was a box of candy. Mine went on the shelf and she told me later that every time she dusted it, she thought of me and how much it meant that I'd saved up to give it to her." He paused. "She told me that for years after. And she'd hug me. A real tight, one-armed hug, pulling me against her. Usually when Jack wasn't around, though I didn't think about that until later. It was a hug just for me that wouldn't hurt his feelings."

Damn, he'd get teary-eyed if he didn't shut up.

"Did she ever find out that Mrs. Browning had to make it under threat from Crusty?"

"If you can ask that, you don't know Crusty at all. Of course he told her his part in it. How he'd been the one to take me shopping. He'd been the one to hunt down the potter at the library and he'd told her she better make a good horse statue. Mom told me later she'd apologized for his behavior and Mrs. Browning had just laughed."

"That she shushed Crusty ups her street cred in my book."

Chuckling, Clint rose. "I'm going to take a shower then I'll take you to dinner."

Listening to his footsteps on the stairs, Rachel laid her forehead on the table. "Aw, crap."

Falling in love with him had *not* been part of the plan.

"It's time." Clint watched Rachel's face go slack as panic set in. They'd set up a time to Skype with the family at the ranch. He was a mix of nervous and excited. "Jack texted. They just finished dinner. Grace and Mike are there, and Kevin. Iris too, of course."

Rachel's face had turned pale. She'd been glowing lately, although he wouldn't foolishly tell her that again. Last time he'd mentioned it, her "glowing" face had turned into a glower right before she'd burst into tears. Fortunately, her crying fits didn't last long.

But he couldn't give in to her tears or fear or excuses. "It's time," he said again.

She nodded, looking as excited as though he'd reminded her of an appointment with the dentist.

He moved to sit closer to her on the couch and cupped her cheek, trailing his fingers around her adorable roundness. Another thing he had the sense not to mention. "Rachel, I have to tell Jack my new address, and he's going to want to know the reason I've moved to Longmont. And it's going to be *fine*. They love you. And me. Our families are going to be excited about our baby."

"They'll be shocked. Uncle Kevin will be disappointed." Her chin wobbled as she fought tears.

He couldn't stand the desperate, hunted look on her face. "I'll give you surprised, but the doc could never stay disappointed or angry, if that's what you're worried about. News of Bingo will supersede any upset feelings about us not telling them sooner."

"Lexi will be hurt. And when she finds out Grace knew,

there'll be the devil to pay."

"And then we keep mentioning Bingo and putting pictures into their heads of a little pink or blue bundle of joy, and they'll forget all about when they found out."

"Real life doesn't work that way, but sure. Since we can't go back in time to tell them a few months ago, let's get this over with."

He chuckled and helped her to her feet. "That's the spirit."

"I don't know what you're so happy about. I'm not sure what Jack will say, but you'll never hear the end of this from Crusty."

He settled her into a kitchen chair and set up the laptop, pulling his chair close so they'd both be in view. "I don't even care about that. I want to shout the news from the rooftops, crowing like a rooster announcing the sunrise."

She giggled. "You talk like a farmer, not a rancher." Her shoulders relaxed and her face regained color. "Roosters crow all day long."

"So will I. Okay, you ready?"

Rachel took a breath. "Yes. But maybe you shouldn't be on-screen at the beginning."

He didn't like that idea at all. This was his baby and his news too. Swallowing resentment, he asked, "Why not?"

"Well, I can ease them into the news about the baby, get

them all happy like you said, and then we can spring the donor part."

Clint shook his head but she kept talking.

"Then when they ask who, how, and so on, you can pop into view."

"Rachel, I'm not a coward, and I'm certainly not letting you face whatever flak comes from this by yourself."

"But—"

"No. Not negotiable." He stared her down, as serious as he'd ever been with her. "If you're not comfortable with it, I'll tell them myself."

Her gaze searched his expression and then she sighed with her entire body. "Okay."

He kissed her cheek. "Atta girl."

Her elbow connected with his chest and he blew out a oomph, glad she'd pulled the punch. He rubbed the area with a teasing frown. "That's going to bruise."

"To serve as a reminder."

He grunted and connected the call. Rachel had set up a time with Lexi and had asked her to position the monitor so she could get a full view of everyone present, instead of talking to them one at a time. Lexi and Jack had invited Grace, Mike, Kevin and Iris for St. Patrick's Day dinner, so Rachel gathering the family wasn't as alarming as on a non-holiday. As the call connected, he squeezed her hand and leaned out of monitor view. Since she'd set this up, maybe he should let her do it her way. "You start with the hello part and then I'll help."

"Thank you."

Once the video connected, Clint felt that familiar pang the sight of home always brought him. The family was seated in the living room, where once he'd "wrassled" with Jack, done homework, and stretched out on the old couch with a book. The couch had been replaced in the past few years, but he could almost smell cookies from his mom's oven. Could almost hear his dad come in from the corral after his last check on the horses before bedtime. Could almost hear the tenderest whisper of goodnight as his mom's knitting needles clicked their own message of love.

"Hey, everyone," Rachel said brightly.

They all answered, and he was both surprised and grateful Crusty and Anna weren't present. The old man might not stick around for a call from Lexi's cousin, but Anna had been quite taken with Rachel at the wedding.

"I'm sure you're wondering why I've gathered you all together."

He smacked his palm to his forehead off-screen. *Way to make everyone nervous.* Rachel swatted his hand under the table, but he leaned into view. "She has a surprise. Me."

Jack broke into a smile and everyone else looked suitably surprised. "What are you doing there?"

Grace and Mike, her husband, looked at each other with open mouths. She turned to the screen first. "It's *Clint*?"

Rachel gasped and drew back as everyone at the Rocking W looked at Grace. "Of course it's Clint," Lexi said. "Can't you see him from where you're sitting?"

"Talk fast," Clint urged Rachel quietly.

"I have something to tell you." She drew their attention back to her. "I've been wanting to do something for a few years, and I've made several attempts to start this…project. And now I have." She took a breath. "I'm pregnant."

"What?" Lexi screeched.

Kevin pulled her back to the couch from her half-rise beside him. "Why don't you tell us everything first, Rachel. Let us absorb this news for a minute before we say anything."

"Well, I was turning thirty, and I didn't have a prospect for a husband in sight, which meant no baby in my near future. And while thirty isn't old, I just" —she shrugged— "wanted a baby desperately. I've been saving for artificial insemination, and I had even suggested starting a family to my last boyfriend."

"Henry?" Kevin's scowl matched Clint's.

"Fortunately, he turned me down."

"Scrawny weasel like that," Kevin grumbled. "You wouldn't have wanted him to donate sperm anyway."

"Right."

Now the family was firmly positioned on her side. Clever girl.

"No, I definitely dodged a bullet there."

Clint leaned forward. He'd be damned if he called himself a sperm donor. He was a dad. "And that's where I come in. I'm the lucky guy who helped her make this baby."

More gasps, some outrage, and two ominously quiet men who simmered with suppressed rage.

"You want to say that again?" Jack growled.

"Yes, yes, I do." Clint had to contain a laugh. That wouldn't make the right impression. "I want to tell everyone, over and over. I'm the father of this baby."

"He helped me," Rachel broke in. "I had money saved for *in vitro,* but it's so impersonal and—"

"Hold on." Kevin's thunderous words silenced the room. "You mean you made a baby with my niece *without* the test tube?"

Rachel nodded, pale once again.

"Yes, sir," Clint answered.

Jack crossed his arms, glower in place. "What the hell, Clint."

"She wanted a baby. I wanted to help."

"I'm sure you did," Kevin said darkly.

Iris took hold of his arm. "Watch your manners."

Everyone looked at her in surprise, probably never having

seen Doc Kevin scolded since his wife passed, a good twelve or fifteen years before.

Iris stared them all down. "That young lady, our niece and sister, has made a decision to start a family. She made that happen regardless of obstacles like not having a significant other. Now she enjoys the miracle of motherhood, and she's bringing us a new family member. I can only be thankful" — she turned back to the screen— "that young Clint Walker volunteered to help her. Certainly a warmer, friendlier way to start a life."

Chest full of emotion, Clint cleared his throat as Rachel brushed away tears. "I'm the thankful one, Mrs. Browning. Rachel chose me, and I plan to do right by her."

"He means," Rachel rushed in, "that he's going to help me out for the first month or so. He's moved in."

He wanted to refute that, to explain he planned to stick around to help her until the baby went to college, as he'd proposed at the outset. Had she forgotten the whole role model idea?

But the family had started with the questions again, so he had to address this twist instead of following up on his own question. "Hold up, and I'll tell you what's going on," he said in a firm, strong voice, just shy of shouting them down. Surprisingly, it worked. Into the quiet, he continued. "I'm working part-time with my advertising firm, part-time on my photography, and part-time selling my photographs for other ad campaigns my company's not in charge of. My L.A. apartment is sublet until my lease runs out. I'll live with Rachel, be here for her and the baby."

The quiet from Montana pulsed through the video screen.

"Seems you've been planning this for a while," Jack said, a dark edge still in his tone, although he had calmed a bit. "Why didn't you tell us before?"

Dammit. Clint could hear the betrayal in his brother's tone. He'd never wanted Jack to feel slighted.

"I wanted to make sure I would carry the baby," Rachel said. "And then, I just... I didn't know how to tell you."

"Rachel." Kevin sighed, shaking his head. "How could you doubt we'd be anything but supportive?"

She sobbed and fell against Clint, but he could tell by the light weight of her in his arms that she was relieved. If these were sad tears, she'd be a dead weight, unable to hold herself upright. The atmosphere in the room eased with Kevin's approval, which had earned him a solid place in Clint's heart.

Lexi perked up. "How long do I have left to make you a baby blanket? What color? What else do you need?" She turned to Grace and Iris. "Oh my gosh. We need to throw her a baby shower."

Rachel laughed and sat up, wiping her tears with her hand. "We don't know Bi—the baby's gender yet, and I don't need a party. Once I get home with the baby, I'll discover what I still need."

She listed the items she had purchased while Jack, Mike and Kevin sat back, seeming to barely listen.

"Stand up," Lexi demanded on hearing the possible due date loomed only three weeks away.

Clint helped with her chair and Rachel had to keep backing up, and backing up, until the women could see her rounded stomach.

"The baby dropped this week. I can finally breathe again." She did a profile, cupping her belly from below, and tears poured down the twins' faces. Even Iris, not yet a family member, had to sniff into a tissue.

"Pregnancy suits you," Mike, Rachel's long-time friend, said. "How much longer will you be able to work?"

"I'm scheduled for maternity leave in two weeks, a week before the baby's due. I don't want to deliver in front of the kids."

The family laughed, but Clint bit his lip. He'd tried, and would continue to try, to have Rachel take more time off. She came home exhausted and napped before eating dinner, then only had two hours in her to do teacher stuff before she fell asleep for the night. If it were up to him, she'd have been on leave right now. But like most of this arrangement, he barely had any say in the matter.

Rachel sat down, once again glowing and wearing a huge smile. "Any other questions?"

Lexi narrowed her eyes. "Yes, I have one." She slowly turned to her sister. "Why aren't you more surprised?"

"Hey," Rachel said with a note of panic, "we'll talk later. Love you all."

She disconnected and turned to him then burst into laughter. "That went pretty well, but I'm glad I'm not Grace right now."

He laughed with her. "Yeah, she's in trouble, for sure." He paused to let the memory of their call linger. "Jack's gonna spit for a while, but your uncle got over it pretty well."

"Yeah. He's one of a kind." She looked at him. "I'm sorry if they put you on the spot. I'd planned to tell them we're not, you know, a couple, but things just got crazy."

Not a couple? What the hell did that mean? "We're having a baby together, Rachel."

"Exactly. That's why we had sex. Why we know each other as much as we do. We were strangers, practically, before. And now, we're the mother and father of this wonderful baby."

He blew out a breath on hearing her acknowledge him as Bingo's father. That need to crow returned. Maybe he'd call Jack later and do a little brotherly repair. Let Jack yell at him a little before Clint could celebrate and they talked about being a dad. Clint had been off to college for Anna's arrival, and outside of foals and calves, he didn't have much experience with newborns.

"And," Rachel continued, making him wonder if he'd missed something she said, "I'm going to appreciate whatever help you can offer when the baby comes. I've read I'll be tired, but I don't want to put too much on you. Let me know if I take advantage, okay?"

His gut went hollow. She didn't talk like she wanted him to stay, like she expected him to. But how could he leave her and the baby after she recovered from childbirth?

Rachel waited a few hours before she called Grace. Clint had taken his gloomy self out for a walk. Had coming clean with his family made the situation too real?

"Can you talk?" she asked when Grace connected.

"Yeah. I'm home. Let me step outside." A door shut. "Okay, I can talk without interruptions from Anita. She's doing homework, but she's been cranky all night. Something about a boy, which makes Mike grump around like a bear."

"My condolences."

"I'll tell her, on both counts. And congratulations on the baby daddy. Good choice, you rat. Why didn't you tell me Clint was your donor?"

"It was awkward, him being Lexi's brother-in-law, and we'd just met, and…" Rachel sighed, pacing the kitchen. "And,

and, and. I can think of lots of reasons, but none of them any good."

"It's fine. I was just surprised."

Rachel held her breath before asking, "And your dad?"

"He calmed down. By the end of the night, he kept saying you'd made a smart decision choosing 'a fine man' like Clint."

Relief made her knees wobbly. "Wow."

"Yeah. I think some of that was Iris's influence."

"Probably all of it. She was something."

"I'll say. So no worries there. This cloud will blow over by tomorrow, and we'll be talking about the baby instead of how he or she came into being." Grace giggled. "I'd love to hear about the baby-making though. I bet Clint's fabo in bed."

Rachel laughed. "Fabo? Did you pick that up in Europe or does that teenager slang come from Anita?"

"You mean he's not?"

"He is, definitely, but that's all I'm saying. Good grief, we have to see him at family celebrations for the rest of our lives. I don't want you speculating."

Grace's end pulsed with silence for a moment. "Just at family celebrations? I thought he moved in."

Rachel felt the weight of all her added pounds and all her years pressing on her. "He did. To help with the baby."

"And that's all? Seeing you together today, I got the impression—"

"No." Rachel squeezed her eyes shut to stave off tears. Damn hormones. "That's all. Just a donor. I mean, he's extremely nice, and he's been so supportive. I can't ask more than that. He's already given me a baby."

"Maybe he wants more. He did move to Longmont."

Rachel slumped into a chair, hand to her belly. "I think this is simply a stop on his way home. To Little Tree. The baby gave him a reason to leave L.A. and the push to start his freelance graphic and photography business. He can put together ads from his own photos or sell his pictures for other commercial uses."

"Which is all great, but he can do that from Longmont. With you."

"He will, for a while."

"Are you sure it's just a while?"

Rachel sighed and tried to ease Bingo's elbow or foot out from under her ribs. A little rub usually helped move the baby to a less uncomfortable position. Not a lot could be called "comfortable" these days. "We talked after we hung up with you guys."

"Thanks for bailing, by the way. Lexi was pissed."

"Sorry. I'm sure she'll get over it."

"I kept a *secret*," Grace said slowly, "from my *twin*. It's going to take a while. But anyway, you talked to Clint afterward, and?"

"And I gave him every opening I could think of to say he wanted to stay around. To be with me. I hinted about us being a couple. I gave him a chance to say I could never take advantage of him because he wanted to be with me. But for him, our relationship is all about the baby. And," she sighed, "I shouldn't expect more than that."

"But do you *want* more?"

Rachel nodded, too cowardly to admit the truth.

"Are you still there?"

"Yes." Rachel whispered the word. Then took a breath. "Yes, I'm here, and yes, I want more. I'm afraid... I'm afraid I've fallen in love with him."

"That's good news, Rachel. What's to be afraid of?"

"I can't expect him to stay. He didn't sign on for the long term. And you know men don't always want to stay around even when it starts out as love, which this did not. Not all men are gems like your dad."

"And not all of them are jerks like yours." Grace's sigh came heavily through the phone. "Rachel. There aren't any guarantees *except* love. It isn't a wedding certificate keeping me with Mike. It's loving him, even when he's grouchy and tired and his family becomes a pain in my backside. Even when I'm pretty sure the Spanish word he calls me is not an endearment."

Rachel chuckled.

"If you're falling in love with Clint, don't let fear step in between you. Don't let the fact that your dad was a jackass—sorry, but he was—don't let the memory of him ruin what's between you and Clint. Give him a chance."

"You say all that like I have a choice, Grace. Love takes two people. And I've never heard Clint say anything about loving me."

"Have you told him how you feel?"

Rachel answered with silence. Of course she'd never said she loved him. There was no point in opening herself to heartache again. She had to be strong for the baby.

"Yeah, that's what I thought," Grace said.

Rachel whispered her greatest fear. "What if he doesn't love me back? What if he doesn't love me enough to stay?"

"Wouldn't you rather know for sure?"

Clint checked the time on his phone. Nine p.m. He called Jack anyway. No doubt his older brother would be waiting for this conversation, regardless of the hour. Walking in Rachel's neighborhood hadn't cooled him down, but maybe Jack could provide some insight. He'd been married twice, after all, and lived with a pregnant woman.

Though Clint doubted he could mark off Rachel's attitude as hormones.

"Clint."

"Jack."

Silence.

"Well," Jack said with heavy sarcasm, "now that we know who we are, what else do you have to say for yourself?"

"I'm not sorry. And I'd do it again."

"Let's not talk about you 'doing it,' okay?"

"Very funny." Clint blew out a breath and paused at a house a few doors away from Rachel's. He leaned against a sturdy fence made of railroad ties. The dark helped him express his feelings. "I'm happy about the baby, Jack. Excited."

"Is this about Sheryl?"

Clint understood his concern. "No. I mean, at first, I did see helping Rachel as an opportunity to step up. Unlike last time."

Jack grunted and Clint hoped they didn't get into that old argument again.

"Does Rachel know about Sheryl, about what's driving you?"

"I wouldn't say *driving me*. But I won't lie; it factored in to my decision. Then I got to know Rachel and..." He shrugged. "It was only about her."

"So this isn't just sex? Not just helping out a—" Jack blew out a laugh. "I can't call her a friend, can I? You didn't know more than her name before the wedding. The first wedding, I mean, to Grace. Who wasn't Grace." He chuckled.

"Come to think of it, little brother, we Walker men have our heads up our asses when it comes to women."

Clint had to laugh, relieved Jack could joke. "You're not wrong."

"So. More than sex?"

"Yeah. I mean, the sex was great, but when she said she wanted a baby… I don't know. Something in me said hell yeah. That should have been my first clue."

"First clue to what conclusion?"

Clint shrugged. "I don't know. That this relationship was going to be more complicated that I'd thought. That I was *in* a relationship already. I couldn't walk away and leave her to do this on her own, with some doctor injecting some stranger's sperm into her."

"What about now?"

"What about now what?"

"Can you walk away now?"

"No." The refusal burst from Clint. He took a breath to calm his voice, keeping the neighbors in mind. "No. And that's the problem. I want to stay in the baby's life."

"What does Rachel want?"

"I don't know. What *do* women want?"

Jack's soft chuckle came through the phone. "And you called *me* a screwed-up cowboy."

Clint remembered. He'd confronted Jack about

"accidentally" marrying Lexi instead of Grace. Now he could sympathize. "These Marshall women really do a number on Walker men, huh?"

"Thank God. Otherwise, I wouldn't have Lexi."

Clint wanted to be as satisfied with life as Jack sounded. "So how do I convince Rachel to let me stay?"

"Tell her why you want to."

Yeah. Right. "If I knew how to put it into words, maybe."

"There are only three words women care about. And if it isn't love driving you, what is?"

Love. Clint swallowed hard. He and Rachel had never said those words to each other. They'd really only been together a weekend here and there. How could he be sure this was love and not just about the baby? "I'm afraid I'll say the wrong thing."

"Just keep talking," Jack said. "Women love a man who tries to explain himself, even if you mess up the words."

"Okay. I'll think about it."

"One other thing." Jack's dark tone caught Clint's attention. "Grace told Lexi that Rachel's old boyfriend is giving her crap about the baby."

Anger boiled in Clint's gut. "What?"

"Yeah. I guess he's a teacher and he's threatened to take her unwed, pregnant status to the school board."

Blood throbbed in his temples, and Clint had to unlock

his jaw before he ground his back teeth to nubs. "When did this happen? Rachel didn't say anything to me."

And why hadn't she? It hurt that she hadn't confided in him. He should know these things, dammit.

"Well, I thought you should know. Not sure if you *should* do anything about it, but…"

The implication hung between them. "But" Jack would do something in this situation. And he knew Clint would too, whether he should or not.

"Thanks, bro."

"Hey." Jack cleared his throat. "Congratulations on the baby."

CHAPTER ELEVEN

Finding out the ex-boyfriend's name didn't take as long as Clint anticipated. He simply asked Rachel.

"Hey," he said at breakfast the next morning, "on the phone with the families last night, you mentioned your ex."

Her immediate grimace warmed his insides. She raised her eyebrows at him in question.

"I just wondered. You never talk about him. His name or where he works or—" Was he being too obvious?

She shrugged. "Henry Lanigan. I'm sure I told you he's a teacher in my building. Fourth grade."

When she didn't volunteer anything else, he nodded. "You considered him as a donor?"

Another grimace. "Luckily he wasn't interested."

Clint took her in his arms and tipped her chin so their gazes met. "A donor like me or a donor in a cup?"

With a soft expression, she laid a palm against his cheek. "No one is a donor like you."

She winked and left the kitchen while he stood still smiling. It took him a minute to realize she hadn't exactly answered his question.

But no matter her initial plan, the jerk hadn't gone for it. Thank God.

After Rachel left for work, Clint got on the school's website and found a picture of Henry Lanigan. Now Clint grimaced. This guy wasn't good enough to be Bingo's father. He had "uptight" and "stern" written all over him. He probably didn't know how to play board games or make up stories or color outside the lines—all things Clint excelled at, thanks to Annabeth. He could even warm a bottle, get a burp out of a baby, and change a diaper if he had to.

He set his alarm and made calls for the majority of the morning, networking and making tentative outreach to some Denver companies. Everyone could offer mountain shots, so Clint pitched some of his California scenery, architecture and candid photos of people, and had a few nibbles by lunchtime. He made a grocery run and threw some stuff in a crockpot for stew. The air held a bit of late spring coolness today, making the hearty dish tempting. Plus, he could be gone for the afternoon and still provide Rachel with a nice meal.

Okay, he meant to show her that his moving in had been a genius idea by running errands and cooking for her. What woman could resist that?

A half an hour before school let out, Clint sat down the block from the elementary school and eyed the teachers' parking lot from his new SUV, with the latest childproof features and a rear-facing baby car seat locked in the seat behind him. As cars picking up children left the premises, he inched closer. Not knowing which door the man would use, Clint had to wait for him out here. Hopefully, the ex hadn't parked elsewhere or left early. And with luck, he'd emerge alone too.

Another half an hour passed, but fortune smiled on Clint as he spotted a man he identified as Lanigan approach a dark Volvo hatchback. He wore a tan jacket and dress slacks. Walking quickly, Clint met him a foot from the vehicle. "Henry Lanigan?"

The man stopped and faced Clint. Bland brown hair and brown eyes flat as a shark's. What had Rachel seen in him?

"Yes?" Lanigan put on a pleasant smile, not committing his eyes to the gesture. "Are you a parent of one of my students?"

"I'm a friend of Rachel Marshall's."

Pale brown eyebrows rose. "Oh?"

"Yeah. I heard you threatened to go to the school board about her baby. Obviously, everyone can see she's pregnant and no one's firing her. So your backstabbing didn't work, eh?"

Lanigan's eyes narrowed. Not a good look on him. "I didn't stab her in the back or anywhere else."

Clint stepped closer. "Good thing. She has friends too. I'm one of them."

"What's that supposed to mean?"

"It means leave her alone. It means don't make me come see you again."

Lanigan shifted, probably not wanting it to appear like a retreat, but he wound up not standing as close as he had been. Clint shifted too—toward him.

"Who's being threatening now?" Lanigan sneered.

Clint held his stare for a long minute. "I am."

April 7th

Rachel only worked for another week before she started her maternity leave a week early. The extra days off now would cut short time with the baby once it arrived, but her tiredness had caught up to her. Her feet throbbed and her breasts ached. She could barely function from wanting to sleep. Truth be told, anxiety played its part too. Despite her doctor's weekly assurances that all looked fine, Rachel worried about having a healthy child and hoped for an easy delivery for both of them.

With the week off, she went through every piece of clothing, every bottle, diaper and box of wipes. She thought through every plan and every detail in every plan.

Nervous, but as ready as she would ever be, she crossed the days off the calendar and waited.

And waited another week.

The baby wasn't late, but with nothing else to do and little energy to do it, Rachel's patience wore thin. Reading fiction didn't keep her attention and non-fiction put her to sleep. Television made her restless and she had to keep pausing any movie she tried to watch in order to rush to the bathroom and pee a teaspoon of drops. With the kid bouncing on her bladder, she didn't know if she urgently had to go or not. Usually not. It didn't help that she'd grown as wide as the Rockies and moved as fast as a glacier.

She struggled awake in her bed with a wet feeling creeping along her thigh. She gave a half-asleep moan. What day was it? She wasn't due to have her period for another—

Her eyes shot open while the rest of her tensed, all thoughts of sleep banished. That couldn't be her period. Her water must have broken.

Oh God. She was having a baby.

Right now. Right here in this bed.

"Clint!"

Clint had moved his stuff across the hall to the guest room to let her sleep undisturbed, but he arrived at her side in a flash.

Eyeing Rachel, he knew this wasn't a false alarm. Her

skin had a pale sweaty sheen, and her expression held both terror and glee.

"The baby's coming."

"I guessed. That's great." A few days early, but that was okay, wasn't it? Wasn't the due date an estimate? "What do you need?"

She bit her lip. "I have to go to the bathroom."

"Okay." He lifted on the sheet to help her out of bed.

Rachel tugged it back. "I'm afraid to move. I think my water broke."

Sweat popped out on his skin. "That happens. If it's messy, we'll deal with it later."

She made a face. "What if I have the baby while I'm on the toilet?"

He chuckled. "Catch it before it drops in."

"I'm serious."

"Rach, I'm pretty sure they don't come out that easily. Not the first time." He didn't have any idea, but mares usually rocked on the ground for a while before dropping their foals.

His comment eased her enough to get up and waddle with her thighs tightly together to the bathroom. When she gave a little shriek, he tapped on the door, heart pounding. "You okay?"

"Yeah. My water's leaking. Just amniotic fluid. Surprised me."

"But you're okay?"

"I think so."

"Are we heading to the hospital?" He had a bag by the door for the trip. Music to soothe Rachel during the wait. Movies to watch. Two different books to read. Baby clothes in a soft yellow, accompanied by one pink hat and one blue hat. Diapers for the baby, snacks for him.

"I'll call the doctor's office in a minute," she called out.

"Are you feeling any contractions?"

"Not yet." The door opened and her beaming face appeared. "I'm sure they're coming. I have an instruction sheet somewhere on what to do now. What to expect."

She waddled back to the bedroom.

"Do you need help getting dressed? Can I make you breakfast? Do you even feel like eating?"

"I don't know if I'm supposed to eat."

"Right." He did the head-smack. Some father he'd make.

Rachel put a hand on his arm. "It's okay. Calm down. Let me call the doctor and get some instructions."

He nodded and sped through the quickest shower of his life. I can do this, he kept telling himself. People had babies all the time, and Rachel would do the hard part.

She asked him to help her into and out of the shower. He watched in amazement as she dried her hair and put on some eyeliner.

When he laughed at her, she said, "Everything else will probably sweat off, but I want to look good in those first photos with the baby."

"You will. You're beautiful."

Forgoing makeup had been wise, since the first four hours of contractions had wrung her out. She doubted she could endure any more pain.

During her sixth hour, Rachel discovered the true reason it was called "labor."

Clint held her hand and sweet-talked her through her contractions. She blew and huffed and cried and even swore, then sighed when each contraction eased. Why had she ever thought this was a good idea?

"Want to go for another walk down the halls?" he asked.

She nodded and he helped her put on her robe. The nurse unhooked her from the monitor, and Rachel felt for the floor with her non-skid slippers before standing.

"I've got you." Clint placed one arm around her back to grasp her far elbow and one hand held her near forearm. No way could she fall, even if her legs gave out.

He was so helpful and kind and sweet to her. He'd called Uncle Kevin and Jack to let them know she'd gone to the hospital. For the past few hours, he'd dried her tears and sweat, told her stories about births on the ranch to distract her, and gotten her ice chips. He'd even helped her to the bathroom and run interference with the nurses who continually wanted to check her monitors—and her cervical dilation. He'd been her support and anchor. She honestly didn't know how she would have gotten through this ordeal without him.

But couldn't he just *go away* for a while?

"Are you ready?" he asked.

Rachel gave him the side-eye but thought better of telling him she'd been walking on her own for thirty years, give or take. She didn't want to be the sitcom version of "woman in labor" who carped at everyone.

Shuffling down the hall, she tried to breathe and stand upright and behave like anyone else in a hospital gown. Her impersonation of a normal patient ended when a strong contraction nearly took her to her knees. Only Clint's support saved her from sagging to the floor. Thank God he was there.

"Are you okay?" His face had turned a little pale under his naturally tanned skin. Creases of worry formed across his forehead.

Having no breath to spare, she nodded and tried to breathe through the contraction. Damn, this one was strong. Once the pain subsided, she ran a hand over her face to wipe away sweat.

"Maybe walking isn't what the baby wants to do right now," she said.

"Let's go back." He matched his actions to his words and turned her in a large arc and headed to her room. One of the women gave him the once-over then shot Rachel a thumbs up. She giggled.

"What's wrong?" he asked, oblivious to the impression he made on the other patients. This hunk of male was so sexy he could distract a woman from labor pains. Or maybe it was less that he was good-looking as him being so solicitous. That was pretty damn sexy too.

As they arrived at the door to her room, another contraction hit. She grabbed the frame for balance and let Clint help keep her upright.

"That wasn't even three minutes." He eased her into the bed and hit the nurse call button.

Rachel summoned a smile. "Maybe it's time."

She grimaced when the little redheaded nurse came in to check her dilation. That woman had the shortest fingers on the planet and a driving determination to get an accurate measurement.

"Oh," the nurse said. "Won't be long now. I'll call the doctor in."

The room became a flurry of activity. Rachel panted and breathed and pushed and held off as instructed. The doctor spoke encouraging words Rachel didn't hear until she said, "One more push should do it, Rachel. Dad, do you want to come down here and witness the birth?"

Rachel tightened her hand on his, panicked. She needed him right where he was.

He cupped her cheek, leaning over to smile into her face as he told the doctor, "I'll catch the next one."

Rachel huffed out a laugh and the baby slid into the world.

"It's a girl," the doctor announced.

Clint smiled at Rachel, tears making his green eyes shine. "Bingo."

"Am I just biased," Clint said half an hour later, "or is this the most beautiful little girl in the world?"

"You're biased," Rachel said with a smile, "but that doesn't make you wrong."

Rachel had snuggled the baby against her for a moment before she was taken away and weighed. The little one earned a healthy APGAR score, and once cleaned up and in a while T-shirt with snaps and a little stocking cap, she was rolled up like a burrito and handed to Rachel to cuddle.

Clint couldn't believe the nurses would just hand them a newborn and leave the room. Rachel had been tended to as well and looked both ready to sleep and to conquer the world. A victorious confidence graced her face now that she hadn't had before.

"She takes after you," he said.

"Am I red-faced and bald?"

"She's not bald. She simply has very, very light hair." He snapped a shot of them as Rachel brushed a kiss on the baby's hair. "I meant that she's beautiful and so are you."

"Oh." Rachel's swiped at her hair. "I don't know about that."

"Then you'll just have to believe me." He took another picture.

"Your turn." Rachel raised her brows at him. "I want to take a picture of you together."

Pleased, he showed her how to work his camera then set it on the bed to take the burrito baby. Fortunately, his hands remembered holding newborn Annabeth and he held his baby with barely a tremor. "So, are we going to put 'Bingo' on her birth certificate?"

Rachel shook her head. "Doubtful. We should have talked about names."

"Do you have one in mind?"

"Juliette."

"Hmm. I like it. Dainty but strong-minded." Clint looked down at the baby sleeping in the crook of his elbow. "Is that from Shakespeare or is it a family name?"

"My mom's middle name was Julia. Maybe we could use a name from your family for the middle name. I mean, if you want to."

His chest went tight. "Thanks. That would mean a lot."

"Juliette Crusty?" she suggested.

He laughed. "Wow. And no. You've had too many drugs."

"Should we rethink Juliette too? I don't want her teased about her Romeo."

"Her friends will call her Julie."

Rachel wrinkled her nose. "Sounds old. I don't think I had any Julies in my year at school. You?"

"Not that I recall."

They sat quietly and Clint gazed at the baby, waiting for inspiration to strike. "What was Sleeping Beauty's real name?"

"Aurora."

"She a bit tiny for such a big name."

"It means dawn."

"Dawn Walker?" He peered at the burrito. "We have to be careful with a last name like that. Lots of combinations don't sound natural. My dad wanted to name his first-born Jonathan. But my mom refused to have a child named after a whisky."

He looked up to share a smile with Rachel and found her staring at her hands. She'd somehow retreated without moving an inch. "What's wrong?"

"I, um… I hadn't thought about using your name."

Her words blasted him in the chest, and he sank back in

the chair, holding Bingo a little closer. Not name the baby Walker? He hadn't even considered another possibility. He was the father and he fully intended to claim the baby as his. To have the baby claim him. He already loved this baby and the suggestion sliced at his heart. "Oh."

"I'm sorry. I didn't intend to hurt your feelings." She gave a helpless shrug. "We should have discussed it, but I didn't realize there was anything to discuss."

"Me either. I assumed she'd be a Walker, but then you also assumed she'd be a Marshall." He took a breath to hold back a tremble. His emotions were in a jumble and he wasn't even hormonal. But he had to say this now. He had to make his feelings clear to Rachel. "I want Juliette to have my name."

"I understand that. I'm torn because I can see both ways making sense. It might be less confusing for her growing up if we're both Marshalls."

"I want you to have my name too. Will you marry me?"

Rachel fought back a sob.

Marry him? He always said the perfect thing.

Part of her wanted to shout *yes!* But how foolhardy and selfish would that be? She couldn't do that to Juliette: expose her to her dad, and then have to patch up the little girl's heart when Clint moved to Little Tree.

Sure, right now while holding a precious baby, it was easy

for him to imagine them as a family. But this domesticity would grow old. Maybe not this week, or even this year, but pretty soon, he'd realize he'd given up his freedom.

Her heart raced. If only she could believe he'd stay.

Juliette came to her rescue by giving out a big yowl—big for a newborn anyway—which distracted Clint. Rachel's breasts tingled, trying to let down milk, and she reached for Juliette to nurse, hoping she had enough milk or colostrum to ease the baby's hunger. Juliette attached like she'd been doing this all her life, which, come to think of it, she had. Such a miraculous event—Rachel's body provided exactly what the baby needed. Or the baby was designed to need what mom could provide. Either way, Rachel couldn't stop staring at the sweet little head and furiously working mouth.

"Don't let her nurse too long." The short-fingered nurse came closer to the bed, having appeared like a shrill chaperone to curtail any bonding.

"She just started," Clint objected.

"And she's probably more than half full." The nurse planted her hands on her hips. "How big do you think her stomach is?" She leaned toward the baby. "You unhook her by popping your little finger in the corner of her mouth."

Rachel twisted away as the nurse reached out, pinkie extended. "That seems unnecessarily mean."

"Do you want chapped nipples? Mastitis?"

Tempted to say yes just to make the woman go away, Rachel bit her tongue. She stroked the corner of Juliette's mouth, and the baby stopped suckling long enough to be eased away. Rachel tucked her breast into her nursing bra.

"This," the nurse said with a smirk, "is when Daddy changes his first diaper."

Clint scooped up the baby into his hands and cuddled her to his ribs like a quarterback. "Not my first."

The nurse shrugged. "Diaper changing between breasts wakes the baby up again so she finishes. If she doesn't suck from both breasts, you'll have to pump out the unused breast or you'll ache for sure and could develop an infection."

Rachel pondered using honey or vinegar on the woman and opted to be a good role model for Juliette. She shot the nurse a huge smile and said in a sweet tone, "Thank you for your advice. I appreciate you sharing your knowledge."

The woman stepped back and gave a narrow, suspicious frown. "It's my job."

Clint returned with a mewling Juliette, who gave the cutest little stretches.

"Better finish feeding her before she starts screaming," the obnoxious woman said.

As though their baby would scream.

Clint scowled but Rachel forced out a "thank you" with another smile.

The woman shifted on her feet. "Yeah, well…"

She left the room with a furrow on her round face, as though she couldn't figure out why Rachel was being nice.

Rachel eased her other breast out and gathered Juliette to her. The baby didn't waste a moment but set in as though she hadn't had a drop to drink in her entire life.

"Does it hurt?" Clint asked Rachel.

She glanced up, wrenching her gaze from the baby. His brow creased in concern, but his gaze stayed glued to the baby. Or her breast.

"Not at all. It's better than being full and waiting for her." Rachel had to keep him from asking her to marry him again. She couldn't face coming up with an answer right now. "When I'm done, or rather, when she's done, I'm going to need a nap."

"I bet." His gaze was warm on hers. "Do you mind if I take a picture of her nursing? You two are so beautiful together. I won't get your nipple or anything, and I won't sell it. This would be just for us."

She doubted anyone else would describe her as beautiful, and especially not right now. A combination of exhausted and exuberant, maybe. "I guess. As long as I can delete anything I don't like."

He already had his camera in hand and was snapping shots. Clint was a total goner for Juliette.

She avoided answering his proposal during their hospital stay, claiming tiredness or using Juliette as a shield. He didn't reopen the conversation, which confirmed her suspicion he'd been suffering from baby-love. Juliette made the idea of a family seem perfect. While hormones raced through Rachel, Clint had probably been hit with the instinctive urge to form a family unit, around since before the caveman. Conditioning as old as time still floated in his brain chemistry.

He was so good with Juliette, Rachel had to fight the temptation to accept his proposal. But that wouldn't be fair to any of them.

She shouldn't have to make such a huge decision in her emotional state. When she thought of him leaving, she cried. When she thought of saying yes, she cried, knowing he'd leave someday. Wasn't it better for Juliette to never know what a great dad she could have had than to have him and lose him later? Rachel had been there, done that. She was saving her child eventual heartbreak down the line.

But, oh, how it hurt Rachel now.

Once home, Juliette had awakened almost exactly every two hours on the dot to nurse. Her little squeaks and mews had quickly turned to heart-wrenching wails about being starved by her mother. For the next few days, the bassinet sat beside the bed where both parents slept. Rachel didn't have the energy to fret about the baby fat hanging around her middle. It would go away or it wouldn't once she started moving around some. For now, she ate enough to be healthy, slept between feedings when Juliette slept, and soaked in Clint's presence.

He was magnificent with the baby. When she commented on it a little enviously, he shrugged. "I've done it before. For the first two years of Annabeth's life, whenever I came home from college, Jack made sure I got acquainted with my niece in all her wonderful and gross aspects."

"Not gross."

"Juliette's not. What she does is natural and healthy."

Rachel rolled her eyes and propped herself up straighter against the headboard. "You've got it bad."

He smiled and didn't disagree. "I'm putting in some laundry. Most of my clothes had spit up milk on them, if not worse. Do you want me to throw in your clothes?"

She considered for a moment. "Do you separate colors from whites? Darks from brights, and all it from reds?"

"Nope."

Her mother didn't raise any fools. "Okay, sure. Thanks."

"You don't have to thank me. That's what I'm here for. Speaking of which…" Clint glanced at the baby sleeping in her bassinet. "I realize I've never told you one of the reasons I volunteered to help you conceive."

She blinked. That came out of nowhere. And sounded ominous. "Why are you bringing this up now?"

"After we told the families about the baby, Jack said he thought you should know. I wasn't convinced, but since you keep thanking me for every little thing, maybe you need to understand why helping you was so important to me."

That *really* sounded ominous. She summoned her courage. "Okay."

Clint settled on the bed facing her. "A few years ago, I was in a serious relationship. We were finishing college when she announced it was time for us to have a baby."

Surprised, Rachel had to bite her lip. Who was she to judge? "What was the hurry?"

He shrugged. "To this day, I still have no idea. We had a fight, and I broke up with her. I didn't want to be manipulated. She…made a couple of bad decisions." Clint took a moment. "Anyway, I didn't step up at the time, and I didn't want to make that mistake again with you."

"But we were practically strangers. You didn't owe me anything. Surely there's more to this story."

He shifted, visibly uncomfortable. "She got pregnant."

Ouch. "I'm guessing, not by you?"

"Not by me. She still wanted us to be a family. I refused." He scowled, looking disgusted at himself. "Just because it wasn't my baby. I was stupid."

Oh God. As Rachel put the pieces together, a leaden feeling invaded her stomach.

Guilt drove him. He hadn't agreed to have a baby with his girlfriend, so he'd volunteered to help Rachel. She could understand his motivation. Didn't necessarily like it, but she could understand it.

Then he hadn't "stepped up" to raise a stranger's baby, so now he was staying to help her raise Juliette. Clint wasn't with her out of love. He meant to right some wrongs from his past.

Still, she had to cut him some slack. "She got pregnant by someone else. Losing faith in her wasn't stupid."

He leaned a hand on the mattress, as though unable to sit upright. "She was injured a bad car wreck and can't have a baby."

Rachel caught her breath, sorrow for the other woman engulfing her. "I'm so sorry, Clint."

"She's still struggling with a lot. Other physical problems from the wreck. Addiction to pain meds."

Her heart broke for them both. "That's terrible. I'm truly sorry for her. Truly. But, Clint, you can't take keep paying for her bad choices."

"I didn't help things. I didn't help *her*." He straightened. "I just wanted you to understand. So, stop thanking me. I'm supposed to be here."

Until he worked off his penance? Because he was still struggling to get over it too. Even as her heart ached for herself, she fell a little more in love with him. What an incredibly good man.

After a week, Juliette slept for three hours. The first time it happened, both Rachel and Clint woke up at the two hour mark and waited. They stared into the dark, their eyeballs glinting in the faint light as they listened to the baby monitor and to the baby sleeping not three feet away. At two hours and twenty-seven minutes, Clint's hand found hers under the covers.

"Do you think she's okay?" he whispered.

For the next thirty-one minutes, they stood crib-side and stared at the sleeping baby, watching the rise and fall of her breaths. When she shifted, they both sighed with relief. At her first little sniffle of hunger, they laughed as Clint scooped her up. Rachel had her breast exposed before she even got seated.

"Are we goofballs?" he asked.

"Of course not. I'm a new mom. I'm supposed to be a little crazy." She grinned up at him. "You're an old pro though. What's your excuse?"

"I'm an old pro at being an uncle, not a father."

"Ah. I guess that distinction gets you a pass."

Once Juliette was fed and changed and fed again, they played with her on the bed, delighting in the baby's movements and expressions. She hiccupped and Rachel looked at Clint. He wore a concerned expression as the escaping air shook his daughter's body.

"It doesn't bother her." Rachel stroked Juliette's face. "I read about this. Babies don't even know they have hiccups. And it's adorable."

"You say that about everything she does."

"So do you."

"I have to. She has me wrapped around her tiny little finger." Clint stroked Juliette's hand. He reached into the basket by the bed and retrieved a toy, which he then held above her. "Don't go to sleep yet, little one."

Juliette's gaze followed the black and white striped fabric ball before she began kicking and waving her arms.

"Good idea," Rachel said. "Can you keep her awake for a while so I can take a shower?"

He frowned. "Sure. But you don't have to ask me to watch her, you know. That's what I'm here for."

Rachel gathered clean clothes and headed across the hall, fully aware that Clint stayed for the baby.

Once clean and dressed, Rachel made them broccoli cheese soup and grilled ham sandwiches. Tomorrow she'd kick this laziness and cook something more difficult. She didn't intend to rely on Clint for everything.

Clint came into the kitchen carrying the baby while Rachel folded the towels he'd washed.

"I was going to do that," he said.

"You've got your hands full."

He glanced at the stove. "You made food."

"I was about to call you down." She left the laundry and removed the sandwiches from the pan.

"I'm here to help you, not be waited on."

She smiled indulgently as she set plates on the table. "You're watching Juliette. You do the grocery shopping and you've made all the meals so far. You washed the clothes and towels. I delivered a baby, but I'm still capable of everyday responsibilities."

He sat at the table, adjusting Juliette to lay across his lap with her head supported in the crook of his elbow. Being a big strong male made his gentleness all the more appealing. It melted her insides every time she watched them together.

They ate and Clint told her about the outside world of the grocery store, the weather, the news he'd seen on TV. She'd caught bits and snatches, but TV didn't appeal right now.

"Would you be up for a walk?" Clint glanced out the window at the weak late-morning sunshine. "It's a little chilly but no wind. We can wrap up the baby. Get her a little sun and fresh air."

Ugh. She needed some exercise but the idea alone was almost too exhausting. "Let's try it. If we stay close to home, we can get her back if the wind picks up."

She changed her clothes and Clint took Juliette to get ready. When Rachel met him by the front door, he wore a baby sling with Juliette tucked into his body. He zipped his coat and the baby disappeared, with only the tiny pom-pom on her hat showing.

Rachel laughed. "So much for sunshine and fresh air."

He went sheepish. "She can breathe. Let's make sure it's okay outside and I'll unzip."

"Nice sling." Rachel put her coat and hat on.

"Oh, it does about a dozen configurations. I can wear her on my back too, up to four years old. That'll free up my hands to take pictures."

Rachel froze. "You've got this figured out."

"Preparation is everything." He opened the door for her.

The sun shone and the birds sang and Rachel frowned in confusion. She tried to process the meaning behind his purchase. He planned to take the baby along when he worked?

A block from the house, he took her gloved hand in his. "Rachel, last week I asked you to marry me. Maybe it's time to make some plans before Juliette gets too much older."

"What's her age got to do with it?" Rachel stalled as her heart thundered in her chest.

"Maybe nothing." He shrugged. "I'm feeling a little bit in limbo."

She looked away. "Marriage was never part of the deal."

He walked a few paces with her without speaking. She couldn't look at him.

"I didn't know you well enough back then to propose. We'd just met. I mean, yeah, we'd had sex too." He drew her to a halt. "But I proposed last week, and I'll do it now. Rachel, will—"

"Don't."

"Why not? I said I'd be a role model for her and support for you, remember?"

Her heart broke but she tried to keep her face impassive. "Let's head back."

Clint cupped the baby. "Yeah, we don't want to stand still or she might get a chill. I think she's asleep."

"I've heard walking around does that, but it's not recommended, at least according to the moms on the blogs. Babies get used to being walked, and then you have to do it all the time or they cry."

He shrugged. "Walking is good exercise. I don't mind. Why are you changing the subject? We were talking about when to get married."

"Slow down, cowboy."

"What?"

She tucked her hands in her pockets. "I didn't say I'd marry you."

He stopped and she had to turn back and face him, trying not flinch under his stare. "What do you mean by that? You want a more romantic proposal?" He made a face. "I guess a hospital room right after giving birth has never been any woman's ideal proposal location. Sorry. I was excited about Juliette being born, but I should have waited."

"The timing of the proposal wasn't the problem." She turned and took a step toward the house, relieved when he followed. "It made sense, in a way. Juliette is a charmer."

He smiled. "Yeah, she is."

"But marriage, Clint? We never agreed to that."

"Then let's agree to a new deal, one that includes marriage." He smiled. "We have a baby and we're living together. This is the next step, right?"

"No."

"What? What does that mean?"

"It means no. There is no next step." She blinked at tears.

"I don't understand."

They'd reached the house and Rachel unlocked the door. She helped him remove the baby from the sling without meeting his eyes. While she'd have liked to lock herself and the baby in her bedroom to avoid his piercing gaze, she owed him a conversation at least. Rachel checked the baby's diaper before she sat on the couch with Juliette snuggled onto her shoulder.

Clint sat facing her, face like stone.

"What we're feeling is natural with a newborn," Rachel said. "I'm full of hormones. You're feeling the baby-love. But that's all this is, and we shouldn't get carried away."

"That's not what this is. I told you last summer when we made her that I'd stick around to help."

"I know. And you have. You are. I won't stop you from seeing her." *As long as you want to.* "I would never do that."

He didn't soften. "So you're not going to marry me?"

She shook her head.

Clint looked away. After a minute, he said, "Then maybe I better find an apartment."

CHAPTER TWELVE

Clint gathered some of his clothes and left, saying he'd be back the next day to get the rest. Rachel watched him go, heart aching.

"Better now than later," she whispered into Juliette's fuzz of hair. She inhaled the smell of the baby's head and felt herself calm. "Trust me on this, sweetheart. I'm saving you heartache down the road."

Rachel went through the motions of making and eating dinner. She changed the baby's diaper mid-feed, taking over Clint's duty. She turned the monitor on its loudest setting. Fear she wouldn't waken when Juliette cried would have kept Rachel awake if she hadn't been so exhausted. She woke as Juliette wiggled against the sheets, but Rachel waited for her to make her first cry. Standing neurotically over the crib wasn't cute when alone. She'd look like a crazed helicopter mom if she woke the baby to nurse.

She took care of Juliette and got through the day. Often she'd turn to talk to Clint or point out a cute thing Juliette did before realization struck. Some tears escaped, some she swallowed down. "I'll get used to being alone. We'll be fine," she told the baby. "Fine. I'll make sure of it."

After her dinner, she had barely finished nursing when someone knocked on her front door. Rachel sighed. Her friends from work had been texting and emailing, wanting to visit. Looked like they hadn't waited for an invitation.

Setting Juliette in her bouncy chair away from the door, Rachel peeked out. And froze. Clint? She swung open the door and stepped back to let him in out of the night. Her spirits lifted. "What are you doing here?"

"Sorry it's late. I've been looking for an apartment. I moved out of the hotel I was in last night, and into an extended stay for the next week."

Rachel soaked in the reality of him. Even after such a short separation, he looked so tall and masculine compared to the tiny human she'd spent her day with. "I didn't know you were coming today to babysit."

His jaw firmed. "It's not babysitting when it's your own child."

Her mouth dropped open. Did men actually feel that way?

"I told you I'd help out," he said impatiently. "Didn't you get my text?"

"Text?" She looked around the room but didn't spot her phone. "My ringer's off. I'm not even sure where my phone is.

It probably needs to be charged."

"Well, why don't you see to that, and I'll take over for you." He spotted Juliette and quickly lifted her into his arms with a soft smile. "Hey, beautiful. How was your day?"

"We've been hanging out," Rachel said. "She nursed well and slept most of the day. Had a couple of normal diapers."

Clint looked over at her without the smile. "I wasn't asking for a report. I'm sure you did fine. I've got her if you want to shower or something."

Chastened, Rachel fled. Sure, she'd welcome a shower, probably needed one, but he didn't have to point it out. She dropped onto the bed and was asleep within minutes.

Two hours later, she came downstairs—showered and dressed, thank you very much—to find Clint explaining baseball rules to Juliette.

"Have you been holding her the whole time?"

He looked up. Briefly. "Yes."

"Babies are supposed to be put down to let them stretch their muscles and discover they're a person separate from their parents."

He stood and put the baby in her arms. "And when it's your turn, when I'm not here, you can leave her by herself. Do you want me to stay tonight?"

Offended by his curt tone, she bit out, "I'll be fine."

He grabbed his jacket and opened the door without

putting it on.

"Thank you for coming," she called quickly.

He gave her a narrow look over his shoulder then closed the door behind him.

Clint came the next day and the next. On the third day, he took Juliette to the grocery store with him. Rachel took advantage of his visits and caught up on her sleep and personal grooming, and began to feel like her old self. Her spirits lifted and her appetite grew.

When he returned, he set down Juliette before he brought in the groceries and put them away. "I took a bunch of pictures. I'll check if there are any good ones and send them to you."

"Thank you. I—"

"Okay, well. I guess I'll head out. I have a lead on an apartment." He kissed Juliette on her head and left.

Upset by his coldness, Rachel gathered the baby into her arms for some comfort. "Your daddy is still mad at me. Or maybe this is our new normal. But even this isn't going to last, I'm afraid. As cute as you are, he's going to get restless."

Her cousin Lexi called that night. They talked about the baby and life in general before Lexi said, "So, Jack said Clint moved out?"

"Yeah. We're fine, me and Juliette. And Clint and I are still friends. He comes by every day to help with the baby."

"Wow. If it wasn't Clint, I'd say that's surprising. But the Walkers are all about family."

"He is. He's all about the baby." Which was the problem. He'd proposed in order to be a daddy, but he'd never said he loved Rachel.

"It's not just about the baby, Rachel. Otherwise, why did he confront your creepo ex-boyfriend?"

She stilled and listened harder. "What are you talking about?"

"Jack told me. He'd overheard me and Grace talking about Henry threatening to go to the school board. Jack told Clint, and Clint went and… I don't know the details, but he set Henry straight."

"Clint never said anything to me. I didn't think he even knew about Henry." She had a vague memory of Clint asking something about her ex. His name maybe? But she hadn't told him about Henry's threats. "When was this?"

"Before Juliette was born. Maybe while you were working with Henry, before you went on maternity leave."

Rachel sank back in her chair, stunned. She must have mumbled goodbyes to Lexi because the call had ended and her wallpaper of Juliette showed on-screen. Her beautiful baby.

She stared until the screen went black. She owed Clint big-time for donating. He'd been nothing but supportive through this whole scheme. Despite moving out, he came every day to see his daughter, still being wonderful and caring and supportive.

Instead of moving to Little Tree or back to L.A., he was searching for an apartment in Longmont. He shopped for her groceries, not wanting Rachel to carry anything heavy yet. While she slept, he did laundry and tidied the house.

He hadn't left her, even when she'd pushed him away. Clint wasn't like her father or her stepfather, but she'd been attributing their traits and their betrayals to him. Waiting for him to fail her.

He never had.

Now she learned he'd gone to bat for her. The idea made her giggle. She'd give a lot to have seen him threaten Henry. Thinking on those days, she recalled Henry practically disappearing in the last week she'd worked. She'd been preoccupied with setting up things for her substitute teacher, and she hadn't paid him any attention.

Clint had erased a huge obstacle in her path to happiness. Before Juliette was born. He'd done it for *her*.

He'd returned to help even after she turned down his proposal, taking care of both of them. Those weren't the acts of a man just caring about the baby and not its mother.

Had she been blind this whole time?

Two days later, Rachel put a lot of work into her appearance and wore her nicest looking post-baby clothes. A rubber band held her pants not-quite together, and these were pants she'd sized up into before she capitulated and bought any maternity stretch pants. The look didn't buoy her confidence. For that, she opted for a royal blue pullover long enough to reach her hips. Bought pre-baby, it stretched over her enhanced bust. She couldn't decide if that looked bosomy and sexy or fat and desperate. Makeup took an effort because she didn't want to appear like she'd made an effort.

Oh hell. She threw her hands up and called it good. Clint knew what she looked like and he'd certainly seen her look worse.

She met him at the door when he came to watch Juliette. He gave her the once-over while he took off his jacket. Did his gaze linger on her chest? Was that good or bad? She couldn't remember being this nervous in a long time. Or ever.

Giving him time to nuzzle the baby, she rushed into speech before he could dismiss her or suggest she go take a shower. "Can we talk?"

"We can. I think we've done it once or twice in the past, haven't we?"

"This is important. Let's sit down." She indicated the couch.

He nodded and sat with Juliette on his lap, his attention straying to her as he let her grasp his finger and gum it.

"I need to explain some things. Some of it you've heard. Some I don't think I've talked about."

"Sure." He looked back at Juliette. "She has such a strong grip."

"Can we put her in her bouncy chair for a couple of minutes?"

His head shot up. Alarm on his face, he asked, "Is something wrong? Is it Juliette?"

"No. No, she's fine. Everything's fine. The family in Montana are all fine," she added to close the subject.

He nodded and eased the baby into her chair. Made out of fabric and attached to a wire base, it allowed Juliette to lay with her head supported. She could kick her legs and bounce securely. Clint swung the mobile over her head so she could make the animals move when she kicked.

"Okay." He took a seat on the couch facing Rachel. "What's up?"

"I want to clear the air. About why I didn't accept your proposal."

His face closed. "We've done this. Let's not rehash it."

"I heard my biological clock ticking when I was twenty-six. My mom had just died and I was alone. Maybe that had something to do with it. She had been my only close family for most of my life." She shook her head. "Uncle Kevin and Grace and Lexi are great, but they live a state away. I wanted to be part of a family again. Not just cousins, as dear as they are. Even a family of two, like I was used to."

She looked at him. Did he hear that? Because of her past, she didn't have expectations.

He had his arms crossed against his chest, not giving her any encouragement, but then, he'd heard this part of the story before. Bucking up her courage, she continued. "My dad and my stepfather both left us, my mom and me. So I didn't search for a husband. I wanted a baby daddy. I wanted to have a baby, someone to love for the long term. I started looking for a candidate, but no one measured up." She swallowed her nerves and looked into his eyes. "Until you."

"I love Juliette, and I was glad to help you out. She's the light of my life, but I want to be more than your baby's daddy, Rachel. I want to be your husband," he said wearily, clearly expecting rejection again.

She smiled. He always said exactly the right thing. "Then I guess you're going to have to marry me."

His face went slack as he searched her gaze.

"Clint Walker." She took his hand. "Will you marry me?"

"Are you sure? I mean, yes." He grabbed her close and kissed her, as though sealing the deal.

Usually his kiss melted her panties, but this one melted her heart. It was a forever kiss. She felt the difference down to her toes.

Better than that, she believed it.

"But *are* you sure?" he asked again.

"I love you."

"Then why didn't you say yes when I proposed?"

"I'm sorry about that. I was being an idiot, standing in my own way. Partly I was exhausted from having the baby, but my doctor cautioned me against postpartum depression." She sighed. "Fortunately you came and took care of us. Kept me in groceries, and let me sleep so I could get back to normal. But there's that other thing."

"What other thing?"

"You never—and haven't yet—said how you feel."

"What? Of course I did." He frowned. "Didn't I?"

She shook her head, breath held. Hopeful.

"I'm sure I said it. I asked you to marry me, after all."

Rachel raised a brow. "Still haven't."

"I think you must have forgotten but" —he rushed on when she tried to object— "I love you. I've loved you from the second or third time we were together. Before I ever heard about the baby plan."

Her mouth dropped open. "You have not."

"I was crushed when I thought you were pregnant and going to spend your life with some other guy. That's when I had the first inkling I loved you."

"Seriously?"

"Why else would a normally sane man agree to be a sperm donor?"

"Because you're such a nice guy."

"Not that nice." He gathered her close into his arms, right where she wanted to be. As his lips touched hers, she felt she'd come home. His kiss sizzled through her. It seemed like forever since they'd kissed.

Long minutes later, she rested her head on his shoulder and felt him kiss her forehead.

"I didn't know you were suffering from depression."

"On the fringes of it, at least. But that wasn't all." She sat up to face him, staying close. Better to get all her confessions over. "I expected you to leave like my dad did. Like my stepfather did. I was devastated by their departures. I couldn't trust a man to stay."

He winced. "And then I moved out."

"But *when* you moved out, I saw you as more than Juliette's dad or my donor. I saw you as the man you prove to me every day that you are. That you're good, and honest, and trustworthy."

He grinned sideways. "I also roll over and play fetch."

Rachel laughed. "Trust me, I see you as a man, not only a companion or baby-maker. Although you do that baby-making really well."

He smiled down at Juliette. "We'll have to space these

kids out. I can only carry one at a time when I'm taking photographs."

She laughed in surprise. "How many kids are you planning on us having? I *am* almost thirty-one."

"You're right. We'd better get started on number two."

She laughed, knowing he'd be around to make lots of babies and help raise them. And, she realized as she gazed in his eyes and saw her own feelings reflected back, he'd be around to love her.

Forever.

EPILOGUE

One year later

Clint looked up when he heard Rachel enter the living room, surprise turning to delight when she eased onto his lap. His arms went around her as automatically as the camera fit into his grip or as naturally as his hands cradled his daughter. He nuzzled Rachel's neck, wondering if he could sidetrack her into a romantic afternoon interlude while Juliette napped. "What's up?"

"There's a job I want to apply for and I thought I'd run the idea by you."

Oh. Serious discussion time. Shoot. He tucked away his disappointment. Being married meant they could always indulge themselves later. "Okay. What is it?"

"It's for a combined second and third grade classroom. Kind of a different setup. It'll be a challenge, but it's a great community. Small town, but nice."

He tried not to let his disappointment show. "So we'd have to move?"

She nodded.

He liked Longmont. Situated near enough to Denver to drum up advertising business, it was also close enough to the airport for any trips he had to make to meet with his part-time boss or other clients in L.A. Working from home meant Juliette didn't have to go to daycare, and they had a sitter for when both he and Rachel had to work. He loved being close to the mountains and all the opportunities for nature shots, which had been more profitable than he'd even hoped. Hiking with Bingo in the backpack carrier made his outings all the more enjoyable. He'd taken a liking to being Mr. Mom.

But if Rachel wanted this new teaching opportunity, he'd move his business again. It was basically an ISP change after all. "A challenge sounds interesting, and I know you'll slay it. Where's this new town?"

"It's a small town, like I said. A place called Little Tree." She grinned.

A flash of joy zipped through him. "What? My Little Tree? In Montana?"

"Yeah. What do you think?"

When should I pack? "Are you sure you'd want to teach somewhere so small? There's limited opportunity for you."

"Are you kidding? I'm going to run that school one day. Probably the entire district."

He grinned, so happy his chest felt as though someone had pumped it up with helium. Cupping the back of her head, he kissed her. "That's for even looking into it. It means a lot that you'd consider moving for me. If you think that's what you want, that you could be happy there, I'd be thrilled to move back."

She nodded. "Both of our families are there, and I want Juliette to grow up with all of her family around her."

"I love you, Rachel."

"And I love you."

After a kiss that almost distracted him from the subject, he said, "If you're sure this is what you want, let's go."

She laughed. "I have to set up an interview date first."

"They'll be lucky to have you."

Rachel sighed and put her head on his shoulder. "I can't think of anything that would make me happier. We're going home."

Clint knew better than to contradict his wife, but she was wrong. Nothing could be better than loving her and their baby, unless it was their plan to add to their family in a few years. He had everything he wanted and everything that could possibly make him happy.

Whether they lived in Longmont or Little Tree or even L.A., in Rachel's arms, he was already home.

Want a free short story in the Love in Little Tree world? Visit my website at megankellybooks.com and sign up for my newsletter. *A Risky Proposal* introduces you to Ryan, the hero of book four, *Coming Home*, but you can read it at any time.

Dear Reader:

Clint and Rachel's story had a long gestation period! Thanks for your patience. By the end, I loved this book so much and hope you did too. Some of the incidents mentioned are personal, some from friends, some overheard in public. You'd be surprised what details some people will offer over coffee. Be careful out there—a writer might be sitting nearby.

If you enjoy my books, I'd appreciate a review posted at your favorite retailer or book review site. I'm not looking for a book report like in school. Just a few sentences will do—but no spoilers please.

You can find my Reader's Group signup on my website (megankellybooks.com) if you'd like to keep up with my releases. I promise not to bombard your inbox.

Thanks so much for reading. I appreciate my readers! You not only put chocolate on my dinner table (wait, did I say that out loud?), but you bring joy to my writing life.

Happy reading!

Megan

Other Books by Megan Kelly

Love in Little Tree series

The Wedding Rescue
Runaway Bride
Baby Makes Three
Coming Home
Ghost of a Chance (novella)

Christmas in Stilton series

Santa Dear

Holly & Ivey

Returning Home Romance series

Fixer-Upper

Harlequin American Romances:

Marrying the Boss

Howard MO series

The Fake Fiancée
The Marriage Solution
Stand-In Mom
(reprinted as No Ordinary Family)

Please visit Megan's website:
at megankellybooks.com

To keep up to date on releases and news, sign
up for her Readers' Group on her website,
or Follow her Author Page on Facebook.

Authors live off reviews and if you liked
this book, I'd appreciate your
honest opinion. Just post it
to your favorite retailer
or a book site like GoodReads.
Thank you.

www.ingramcontent.com/pod-product-compliance
Lightning Source LLC
Chambersburg PA
CBHW070854180626
46817CB00003B/769